"Who are you?"

Her voice was breathless. "You're a sailor, aren't you? Or a fisherman with a boat anchored offshore somewhere. That's why no one has heard of you. Isn't it?"

He smiled. His fingers spread over the side of her face, threading into her hair. "Is it?"

Molly tried to swallow, but her throat was too dry. "Why won't you answer me?"

"Why do you want to know?"

"Because," she said. His fingers slid down to her throat and where he touched, electric pulses of pleasure throbbed. "Because I think you're going to kiss me and I'd like to know who you are first."

"But wouldn't it be fun, just once, to be kissed by a stranger?"

His breath infused her, dizzying, intoxicating. His lips touched hers, as soft as a whisper. It was a kiss like no other she'd known. He tasted of hot wet nights and the sea. There'd never been a moment of purer, all-encompassing pleasure in her life, and as long as she was in his arms, captured in his spell, she didn't want to know anything else....

Dear Reader,

You asked for it. You got it. More MEN!

The four sexy, extraordinary men we brought you in the MORE THAN MEN quartet were so irresistible, that we're bringing you some more. Just as before, whether their special powers enable them to grant you three wishes or to live forever, their greatest power is that of seduction.

So turn the page—and be seduced by Sean. It's an experience you'll never forget!

Thanks for your letters—and be on the lookout for upcoming MORE THAN MEN books.

Regards,

Debra Matteucci
Senior Editor & Editorial Coordinator
Harlequin Books
300 E. 42nd St.
New York, NY 10017

Harlequin Books

TORONTO • NEW YORK • LONDON
AMSTERDAM • PARIS • SYDNEY • HAMBURG
STOCKHOLM • ATHENS • TOKYO • MILAN
MADRID • WARSAW • BUDAPEST • AUCKLAND

ISBN 0-373-16538-2

KISSED BY THE SEA

This edition published by arrangement with Harlequin Enterprises B. V.

Printed in U.S.A.

Chapter One

Molly Blake stopped her car in front of the weather-beaten little cottage and stared at what was to be her home for the next six weeks.

"You have got to be kidding."

Awkwardly, she clambered out of the car, balancing on her right foot and cursing under her breath while she fumbled in the back seat for her crutches. A week with a broken ankle and she still wasn't used to depending on a set of sticks to get around.

Delilah, the one-hundred-thirty-pound Irish wolfhound who had shared the trip from Philadelphia with her, picked her way delicately across the front seat, paused at the open door to sniff the air, then turned around and resumed her seat—apparently suggesting the best course of action would be to keep driving and hope for better things.

"I'm with you, girl," Molly said, and, with a grunt, released her crutches from their entanglement beneath a discarded windbreaker, an unfolded map and a paper sack of fast-food wrappings.

She took a few steps up the shell-encrusted walk, hoping the view would improve with proximity. It did not.

When Hal, her managing editor, had offered her the use of his family's beach house while her broken ankle healed, Molly had been reluctant. She was a woman of action and she needed to be where the action was. She had half a dozen stories under development and some ongoing investigations that wouldn't keep. But after five days of trying to keep impromptu assignations with informants while hopping along on one leg and trying to flag down taxis with her crutch, Molly was forced to admit it was time for a break. Maybe organize her papers for that book she'd always intended to write. And after a suffocating summer in the city, autumn at the seashore did sound nice.

She had pictured a graceful curving structure of cedar and glass, overlooking azure sea and sky. Floor-to-ceiling windows to admit a billowing sea breeze. Sundecks. A Jacuzzi.

From the looks of this place, she would be lucky to find running water.

It was ancient. The wood siding was rotting, the porch roof propped up by a two-by-four, the windows encrusted with grime.

But the sun was setting and the nearest motel was thirty miles back down the road. And, she had to admit, her ankle was throbbing like crazy. Surely the place couldn't be as bad on the inside as it looked on the outside.

"I'm going to get you for this, Hal," she said as she proceeded up the walk at a clumping gait.

There was a rust-encrusted iron gate across the path, surrounded by a thick viny plant that was now out of bloom. When she nudged the gate with her crutch, it promptly tumbled off its hinges and onto the ground. Molly kicked it aside with her crutch.

There was a moment of hope when the key Hal had given her wouldn't turn the lock on the front door. Maybe she had the wrong house, after all. Maybe if she drove another block or two...

No such luck. She had passed the Harbor Island Bridge ten minutes ago and it was impossible to get lost from there. The sign swinging from the post at the driveway, stained and weather-beaten as it was, clearly said, Gull Cottage. She was in the right place, and when she applied the weight of her shoulder to the door and forced the lock, it swung open with a creaking, scraping sound. The momentum brought her over the threshold and she grasped the crutch quickly, flailing for balance.

She righted herself and looked around, trying not to expect too much. She wasn't disappointed.

"It might be a little...dusty," Hal had said vaguely. "I don't think anyone has been up there in a while."

A while? How about a decade? Every piece of furniture was covered with dingy white cloths, and what the dustcovers did not conceal, the cobwebs did. There was one small room, with a loft overhead, a tiny bathroom to the left and a kitchen to the right. The only interesting feature was a row of portholes high on the wall facing the ocean, but a large plate-glass window and a set of double glass doors beneath them made the wall look lopsided. Both the portholes and the window were distorted by a buildup of saltwater and the pitting effect of blowing sand, and the light they allowed in was filtered and weak.

Molly sought the main circuit breaker, ambling among the spooky shrouded shapes and grimacing at the sticky feel of the closet door beneath her fingers.

She threw the switch and was relieved when an overhead fixture—a hanging lamp shaped like a ship's wheel—sprung to light.

Delilah stood at the threshold, poking her slender canine head around the corner as though questioning the wisdom of proceeding farther. Molly looked at her sourly. "Coward."

She started jerking off dustcovers and piling them in the center of the floor, raising such a cloud that she was coughing and gasping before she was half finished. The activity seemed to resign Delilah to her fate, and the dog cautiously ventured inside and began to explore her surroundings. And there was a great deal to explore, Molly discovered when the dust cleared.

The furniture was an eclectic mix of chipped green wicker and maple castoffs, and every available surface was stacked with books. An additional set of bookshelves flanked the brick fireplace, which someone with dubious taste had painted white, and they were crowded three deep with more dusty leather-bound volumes. Seashore memorabilia cluttered the mantel and the windowsills. But the most interesting item was on the dark oak wall above the fireplace—a painting of a man riding a dolphin. Though the canvas was too grimy and dark to gauge the quality, the man's face was striking. All around the smell of mold and age permeated the air and the overall impression was dank and oppressive.

"Talk about atmosphere," Molly murmured, and made her way toward the kitchen.

The good news was that there was running water. The bad news was that the water was rusty and the pilot light on the stove was out. After five books of matches and an uninterrupted string of colorful expletives, Molly gave up on trying to light it. She was hot, dusty and out of patience.

She had pictured herself spending this evening sipping a glass of wine on the deck overlooking the ocean as a rich cerulean twilight fell. She had forgotten to pick up wine, there was no deck and twilight was fast fading away. But she had driven over two hundred miles to see the beach, and she was not going to close her eyes on this day until she had seen it.

Delilah was waiting at the door, either reading her mistress's mind or as equally anxious to get outside into the fresh air. Molly struggled for a moment with the balky double doors.

She could hear the surf sighing and pounding, and she could taste the seawater in the air. The ocean itself, however, was completely obscured by a bank of thick fog that had arrived with the fading of the day. Tendrils of it caressed her cheek and drifted past her like smoke, and the closer she looked toward the ocean, the soupier it became.

She stood there for a moment, her lips pressed together in a thin tight line, and gazed out into absolutely nothing. A perfect end to a thoroughly disappointing day.

Abruptly, she swung forward on her crutches. "Come on, Delilah," she said. "We don't have to take this." She had come here to see the ocean, and see it she would.

She started down the sandy boardwalk that led to a wooden staircase to the beach, Delilah trotting ahead with her nose attuned to the smell of the sea.

There was a little wooden platform at the end of the boardwalk, and Molly definitely did not like what she saw from it. The stairs were much steeper than she had imagined, following a rocky path down the cliff toward the sound of crashing surf—which she could hear quite clearly now, but still couldn't see. For a moment, her courage wavered—she could barely negotiate the crutches on level ground—but then she chided herself. *What did you expect? This is Massachusetts, not Florida. In New England there are cliffs.*

Drawing a breath and squaring her shoulders, she started down.

At first, Delilah trotted ahead, nose to the ground, tail wagging. But as the incline became steeper, the visibility less and Molly's progress more uncertain, even the dog seemed worried and stayed close to her mistress's side. Eventually, the fog was so thick that Molly literally could not see the next step, and had to feel her way along with her crutches. The ocean roared in her ears and she could feel the moisture weighing down her short curls and congealing on her eyelashes.

"You are really stupid," she told herself. This was not the first time she had heard that statement in the past week. She had broken her ankle, after all, while running after a moving car that was transporting a certain senator from whom she was determined to get a statement. She might have caught it, too, at the next red light, had she not slipped in an oil-slick puddle...and that street, she recalled, had not been nearly as slippery as these steps.

A sensible person would have given up. Molly, however, had never been accused of that. Besides, it would be no safer to turn around than to continue down.

Suddenly, Delilah gave a low growl that ended in an ear-shattering bark. Startled, Molly swung her crutch forward—and missed the step completely. She pivoted desperately for an endless second on her other crutch before her own weight carried her forward. Her stomach lurched sickeningly as she felt herself tumbling over into the bottomless fog.

And suddenly her fall was broken by a force so solid, the collision knocked the breath out of her lungs. Something had her around the waist and was dragging her backward. Delilah was barking furiously. Molly would have screamed if she had had any breath at all, and it was perhaps fortunate that she did not because before she knew it, she was on solid ground again. When her breath did return, all she could do was gasp.

The force she had encountered was a man's chest; the arms that were wound around her so firmly had saved her life, not threatened it. Even Delilah's frantic barking had settled down into an uncertain cross between a whine and a growl. Molly clung to her rescuer and tried to recover her composure. That was much easier said than done.

Her head was spinning, her heart was pounding and the swirling, drifting fog created an eerie one-dimensional world in which she couldn't entirely trust her senses—any of them. Her savior said nothing; he simply held her pressed tightly against a body that was warm and sleek and muscled, and looked down at her with eyes that were the most mesmeric shade of sea green she had ever seen.

Later, she would wonder how she could have seen the color of his eyes when the fog was so thick and the light was so poor she could barely see his face, a mere six inches from hers.

But what a face it was. High forehead, full lips, rich dark lashes, exquisitely sensual yet boldly, almost shockingly masculine. It was the kind of face that, once seen, was not easily forgotten, and that was why Molly stared at him so overtly—there was a moment when she was convinced she *had* seen him before.

He had thick ebony hair, shot through with streaks of silver, which fell in wet waves to his collarbone. His neck was strong and columnar, his shoulders broad and glistening in the subtle, foggy light. His chest was completely bare, smooth and hairless and tightly muscled. He had caught her against his side, and Molly could feel his hip and the length of his thigh pressed against hers. She could feel the wetness of his skin through her shorts, and the shape of his muscles. She could not detect any sign of swimming trunks.

Clinging to him, she looked up into his eyes and, before she could stop herself, said with a gulp, "You're not wearing any clothes, are you?"

A faint upward curve softened his lips. "You're not hurt. Good."

His voice went through her like the chords of a harp, sweet, sensuous, melodic. It rippled through her nerves and tantalized her senses as surely, as erotically, as a caress. For a moment, she was able to do nothing but stare at him, breathless and dizzy, and wondering, for a wild irrational moment, whether any of this was real.

She could hardly be blamed, after all. The fog, billowing and stretching like the backdrop of a Gothic novel, the sea crashing in the background, a completely naked man saving her life . . . Anyone might wonder.

But Molly Blake was not anyone. She was Philadelphia's foremost investigative reporter. If there was one thing she had never doubted, it was her grasp on reality.

She took a small, wobbly though determined step backward, trying to look at him with a more objective eye. It wasn't easy. The Greek-coin profile, the wavy wet hair, the athletic flow of neck into shoulders . . . this was not the kind of body one encountered every day. And it was almost impossible to keep her eyes above his waist.

She cleared her throat a little, determinedly fixing her eyes on his face. "Where did you come from? That is—I'm awfully glad you did, but—Where did you come from?"

He made a graceful gesture downward, one hand still holding her arm to steady her. "The sea," he replied simply. "This is a dangerous walk in such weather. You really should be more careful."

The sea? she thought incredulously. What kind of man would go swimming on a day like this?

"Yes. You're probably right. The fog came in rather suddenly."

A little lie, but she didn't care. The grip of his fingers on her arm was gentle but strong, a quiet support that made her feel safe from everything. And she couldn't help it; she let her eyes drift, briefly and circumspectly, below his waist. The fog was like a gauzy blanket, concealing a great deal and hinting at much more. She had an impression of a flat abdomen, the tight plane of his hip, lean bare thighs, and was tantalized by the promise of the rest. She swallowed hard and looked up at him.

"Well, thank you for breaking my fall. I should probably go back now."

"Yes," he agreed. "I'll walk you up."

He started to release her arm but she clung to him, hopping on one foot to maintain her balance.

"You *are* hurt," he said, concerned.

"No, it's just that...well, I had a pair of crutches when I came down."

His eyes moved over her in quick assessment, and although she knew he couldn't possibly see any more of her than she could see of him in the soupy fog, he seemed to take in her entire situation at a glance.

He gave a soft whistle and Delilah crept up, still growling low in her throat.

"It's okay, girl," Molly said. "He's one of the good guys." And, because one can never be too careful, she added meaningfully, "So far."

He smiled and placed her hand on Delilah for balance.

"Fine dog," he commented. "I'll get your crutches."

He turned and disappeared into the fog.

"Wait," Molly called. "It's okay—you can't possibly find them in this fog! Be careful!"

But almost before she had finished speaking, he was beside her again, her crutches in hand. Delilah greeted his return with a short bark that ended in a whine of submission as she extended her head to be petted.

Molly took the crutches with a mumbled, disbelieving thank you. But as she struggled to fit them under her arms, she was suddenly swept off her feet and into his arms.

"You'll be much safer this way, I assure you," he said, and started up the stairs.

"No, please, you don't have to. I can walk, really."

Her protests were breathless and not very convincing, mostly because she couldn't quite believe what was happening. This beautiful, naked, Greek god of a man was carrying her in his arms through the fog-swept night. Really, things like that simply didn't happen to her. Besides, he'd give himself a heart attack, carrying her up all those stairs, if he didn't lose his footing and send them both plunging onto the rocks below first.

"No trouble at all," he replied in that smooth, musical voice. He wasn't even winded.

He moved up the narrow, almost invisible steps with effortless grace, carrying her as easily and as securely as though she were a baby. There was something elemental and innately sensual in the entire experience: the feel of his wet skin and rippling muscles, the salty tasting fog and distant surf, being borne helpless in the arms of a stranger. It would have been as perfect as a poem had not one of the principals been Molly, who, in rumpled shorts and baggy Phillies T-shirt, clutching her crutches to her chest and trying to keep her plaster-encased foot from striking him in the arm, felt about as romantic as a troll.

"Umm . . . I don't mean to keep bringing it up," she said, "but you really *aren't* wearing any clothes, are you?"

He looked down at her with a pulse-stopping grin. "You do seem to be somewhat fascinated by the subject, don't you?"

"I don't mean to pry, but most people do wear swim trunks, at least."

"Do they? And what do you wear when you swim?"

"I don't swim."

"Pity. You're missing one of life's greatest pleasures."

They had reached the top and he set her down gently, waiting until she had full control of her crutches before releasing her. "There," he said. "Your noble canine will see you the rest of the way home. Good night, Molly Blake. Try to be more careful, will you?"

"Wait!" She pivoted on one crutch as he started down the stairs. "How did you know my name? I didn't tell you."

His smile was as dismissive as a shrug, but twice as enchanting. "It's a small town." He touched two fingers to his forehead and once again turned to go.

"Wait," she called again, and was unable to account for the urgency she felt, her reluctance to let him go. "You didn't— That is, what's your name?"

There was only the slightest hesitation, then he replied, "It's Sean. Sean Seaward."

"Will I see you again? I mean—" She tried to defuse the desperate sound of that with a joke. "How will I know where to send the thank-you card?"

Again he grinned, and lifted his hand in a wave. "Oh," he assured her, "I'm easy to find."

A breath of a breeze pushed a deep bank of fog between them. Molly lifted her hand to brush it away, to keep her eyes on the man. But he was gone.

MAYBE IT WAS the fog or even the bizarre encounter with the stranger, but when she returned, the cottage looked cozy somehow. Suddenly she didn't want to do anything to destroy the atmosphere.

Instead she ate a cold supper and made her bed on the green wicker sofa. Thinking about the man on the steps, she drifted off to sleep.

Sometime during the night, she awoke with a start. She knew where she had seen him before.

She swung her feet to the floor, almost tripped over Delilah, fumbled for her crutches, knocked over a lamp in her haste. She righted the lamp and clumped over to the fireplace.

"Aha!" she exclaimed softly.

In the painting over the fireplace, a magnificent dolphin crested a stormy wave with a man astride his back. The rider held up one muscled arm in triumph while his long ebony-and-silver hair streamed behind him, green eyes alive with a lust for life. It was a stunning portrait, captivating and disturbing with its stormy colors and Rembrandt-like use of ambient light. But it wasn't artistic appreciation that caused Molly to catch her breath in sudden excitement; it was the subject matter. The rider of the dolphin was none other than the man she had met tonight.

The signature on the painting was clearly readable in the lower left-hand corner: Sean Seaward.

The date below the signature read 1894.

Chapter Two

Molly had never been able to resist a mystery. If it hadn't been for Sean Seaward, she would have been on her way back to the city before first light, her head ringing with invectives and bent on vengeance against Hal and his easy generosity. This, however, put a new slant on things.

Sean Seaward, naked on the beach steps. Sean Seaward, posing for a self-portrait in 1894—a portrait that just happened to hang over the fireplace of the house in which *she* was staying. Just what kind of game was this fellow trying to play? It *was* awfully coincidental that he had shown up just in time to save her from a dangerous fall. But come to think of it, she wouldn't have fallen if Delilah hadn't started barking... and it didn't take much imagination to realize what, or who, had spooked the dog in the first place.

So she slept as comfortably as the wicker sofa allowed, until Delilah woke her up some time after nine. She let the dog out and sleepily made instant coffee from one of the packets she always kept in her purse. She stood in front of the fireplace and studied the painting.

In the morning light, the resemblance was even more astonishing. The dark, romantically streaked hair, the sharp profile. The lean bare chest, tautly muscled arms, the spare waist—all unnervingly familiar. Splashing waves and swirling mist concealed the more personal parts of his anatomy, but glimpses of his bare legs and the long line of one hip were visible in the painting.

Having met him, she could very well believe he was an artist's model, but an artist? Somehow that did not seem quite so right.

What bothered her more was the coincidence of having met the man within hours of her arrival. Had he been spying on her? Watching the house, waiting for her to leave? If so, why? And what was that nonsense with the date? She examined it closely, standing on tiptoe. It read 1894. No mistake; it was clearly written in the same dark red paint as the signature was inscribed. Was it some kind of joke?

No doubt the whole thing was perfectly innocent, and another person would have filed the story away to be pulled out at cocktail parties when conversation lagged. Not Molly Blake. Her reporters' instincts were sharpened; she couldn't walk away until she at least checked it out. When on the trail of a story, she had been likened to a shark with the scent of blood, and in many ways the description was apt. The allure of an unanswered question was at least as compelling, and the ruthless determination with which she pursued her answers could, she had been told, be compared to a feeding frenzy.

She did not expect this particular hunting trip to take more than a couple of hours out of her morning. By lunchtime, she would be on her way home—with, perhaps, an overnight stop in a nice motel to compensate for her trouble. And she would get even with Hal if it took the rest of the year.

The first thing she needed was a telephone directory.

But no such thing was to be found, she discovered after only a few moments' search—and for a very good reason. The cottage had no phone.

"Great," she growled, and let a stack of dusty books and magazines fall back into place on the old sea chest in front of the sofa. She caught a glimpse of some of the titles, and couldn't help being intrigued: *Mysterious Creatures of the Sea, Legends of the Deep, Sea Serpents and Mermaids.* But the title that caused her to stop and stare was *Myths and Legends of Coastal New England.* For on the cover of the book was a reproduction of the painting that hung over the fireplace.

"What the...?" She scooped up the volume and sank heavily to the sofa, her plaster-wrapped foot extended straight out before her. She opened the book and searched for the cover credit.

The Sea King by Sean Seaward, 1894. *The Sea King* is in a private collection.

"This is too weird," she mumbled, looking from the painting over the fireplace to the cover of the book. "What is going on here?"

She started to thumb through the book. Delilah barked once, sharply, at the back door, wanting to be let in. Molly got her crutch and hobbled toward the door, still studying the book.

Delilah barked again and Molly said, "All right, all right, I'm—"

She swung open the door and broke off. Standing before her was the man of the hour, Sean Seaward himself.

He was wearing white cotton pants with the cuffs rolled up, a white shirt unbuttoned over his bare chest and deck shoes with no socks. His hair was jet black, streaked with several wide bands of silver, crinkly in the way of people who spend a lot of time in the water. His skin was golden, his eyes brilliant green. He was not a figment of her imagination or an incredibly brilliant dream. He was, unmistakably, the man in the painting. He was, unmistakably, the man she'd met last night.

He was, unmistakably, as real as anything could get.

Delilah grinned and wagged her tail, looking proud of her acquisition as she squeezed her way past him and into the house. Sean Seaward smiled. "Hi," he said. "Remember me?"

That voice. Oh, yes, she remembered. Rich, sensual, sweetly evocative... there was no mistaking that voice. But the words he spoke, casual and easy, were hardly those one would expect to issue forth from the mouth of the "Sea King."

And all Molly could think of to say was, "I see you found some clothes."

His eyes moved over her figure, naked except for the thin sleep shirt, in a way that made every inch of her skin tingle. He replied equitably, "I see you lost some."

Molly resisted the impulse to cross her arms over her breasts, but could not completely control the heat she felt creeping up the back of her neck.

He lifted the basket he held in his hands and added, "I brought you a little welcome-to-the-neighborhood present. May I come in?"

"Oh... well, yes, of course." She backed away from the door and he stepped in. "Neighborhood? Does that mean you live around here?"

"More or less."

He turned unerringly toward the kitchen and Molly, dropping the book onto a table after one more quick look at the cover, hobbled after him.

"What does that mean, more or less?"

As he walked, he looked around. "You've certainly got your work cut out for you, haven't you? How long are you planning to stay?"

"About twenty minutes. Listen, I'm really glad you stopped by. I wanted to ask you—"

But her words were drowned out by the clatter of shells against porcelain as he tipped the basket open into the sink. Oysters, clams, lobster, crabs and shrimp spilled out, almost filling the sink. Molly gave a little squeak of alarm as she saw some of them were still moving.

"What is *that?*"

He glanced over her shoulder and gave her a grin that actually made her pulse flutter for just a second. "Lunch—or at least the makings thereof. If you'll point me to a stew pot, I'll get started."

Molly tried to disguise her distaste. "Lunch? I haven't had breakfast yet."

He seemed surprised. "The sun has been up half a day."

"For you, maybe." She fixed her eyes dubiously on the contents of the sink. She was quite certain she was not up to decapitating shellfish at this hour of the morning—or even watching while he did it. She took a cautious step backward as something shifted and rattled its shell against the basket.

"Um, listen, this was really nice of you but—"

"No trouble at all." He opened drawers until he found a knife, and held it up to the light to examine the blade. "But I really should get this on to simmer if you're going to eat it today." He picked up a lobster, the antennae waving in his hand.

"Uh, right. Excuse me, I have to feed the dog." She left the room as hurriedly as anyone on crutches could reasonably be expected to do.

In the living room she paused to rummage through her duffel for a pull-on skirt—which, with the exception of a couple of pairs of extremely large shorts, was the only kind of clothing she could get on over her cast—and a cotton sweater. She went into the bathroom, with its claw-footed tub and circular shower rod, to change.

Her thoughts were racing, lining up questions for interrogation, speculating on the answers and, yes, enjoying the excitement of his unexpected appearance on her doorstep. First, the mysterious hero of the night, rising from the sea to save her life, then immortalized in oils a century before...now taking over her kitchen with a basket of seafood and a cheery "welcome to the neighborhood." Who *was* this man?

He even sounded different. Not his voice, which was one thing she was sure he could never change or disguise, but his manner of speaking. Last night, his tone had been stilted, even formal. Today, his manner was easy and relaxed, almost colloquial. It was as though he had somehow divined her suspicions and had determined to put them to rest with the good-neighbor routine.

Which was interesting, because even Molly didn't know what her suspicions were. All she knew was that whenever a man appeared to step out of a hundred-year-old painting to save her life, she felt more or less obligated to ask a few questions.

The skirt she pulled on was long, gauzy and romantic, and the loose cotton sweater created an eclectic, arty look that she didn't entirely hate. Normally a jeans-and-boots kind of girl, Molly had scavenged her vacation clothes from the closets of her friends. She hadn't even packed a single bra—and wasn't the least self-conscious about it. At this stage in her life, comfort was more important than appearance—even if there was an incredibly good-looking, highly intriguing man in the next room. Besides, her figure was pretty good for a woman of thirty who had never set foot inside a gym and whose idea of healthy eating was not adding salt to her french fries.

She brushed her teeth and ran a comb through her short back curls. Scrutinizing her efforts in the cloudy mirror, she actually pinched her cheeks for added color before she caught herself. What *was* she doing? She was supposed to be interrogating the man in her kitchen, not dating him.

She clomped back out to the living room, aware that whatever effect might have been achieved by the outfit was completely ruined by the cast and crutches. She could hear cozy domestic sounds from the kitchen—pans rattling, silverware clinking—and smell an onion broth. It occurred to her that leaving a mysterious stranger alone in her house with a roomful of butcher knives was not the smartest thing she had ever done, and her lips tightened dryly. Maybe Hal was right; she was overdue for a vacation. She was in serious danger of losing her big-city edge.

Nonetheless, she took her time hobbling to the front porch, where she had left the dog food last night, dishing out the kibble, freshening the water and calling Delilah to the feast. Then she squared her shoulders—figuratively if not literally—and went inside, prepared to do battle for the truth.

She didn't have far to go. He was standing in the living room, hands in pockets, head tilted back slightly as he looked over the dusty beams and sagging balustrade. He glanced at her with a friendly smile.

"Interesting old place, isn't it? No one's been here in a while, though."

Molly made a noncommittal sound and came forward casually. He was standing in front of the bank of windows, and with the morning light behind him, the shape of his legs and buttocks—as perfectly formed as she remembered from the night before—were clearly visible. She could not discern a trace of underwear...not, of course, that she tried.

"So, John." She waited half a beat for him to react to her calling him by the wrong name. He didn't appear to notice. "You're an artist's model?"

With a puzzled expression, he looked up from the collection of seashells he was studying. Molly gestured to the painting over the fireplace, and the puzzlement dissolved into a chuckle. "Oh, that."

Oh, that? She had expected a somewhat more dramatic reaction. He had barely even glanced at the painting. Instead, he moved away, and cranked open one of the windows that flanked the door.

"You'll enjoy the sea breeze," he said, "and the room needs airing out. Of course—" he paused as the handle came off in his hand "—the place needs a little work. Who owns it now?"

Molly was still so startled by the neat way in which he had evaded her question that she almost missed his. No one wriggled out of one of Molly Blake's interviews that easily.

"Um, a friend of mine, back in Philadelphia," she said. "My boss, you might say."

"Philadelphia? Is that where you're from?"

She noticed the way his eyes moved over her figure as she swung across the room. It made her want to stand up a little straighter and move a lot more gracefully. Impossible with these crutches attached to her.

"That's right. Have you ever been there?"

He just smiled, and turned back to reattach the handle. "No. What kind of work do you do, Molly?"

The sun, streaming through the open window, glinted on that oddly streaked, silken-textured hair of his and distracted Molly so that for a moment she forgot to be annoyed. *She* was supposed to be asking the questions, after all.

"Look, Sean..."

He looked up and Molly had to remind herself that this was not, after all, an interrogation—just a couple of neighbors getting to know each other. If he was a neighbor. And if she wanted to get to know him. So she added innocently, "That *is* your name, isn't it?"

He just smiled. She was forced to ignore her frustration and plunge ahead.

"I'd really like to know more about that painting."

"What painting?" Then, "Oh—"

She echoed with him, "That."

He grinned, turning back to his work. "What do you want to know?"

"Well, for one thing, why is the date on the canvas 1894?"

"Perhaps that was when it was completed."

"Didn't you just tell me *you* sat for it? Now, I can believe a lot of things—"

"I'm sure I didn't tell you that," he interrupted, testing the handle. The window opened fully and he stepped back with a satisfied nod. "That should do until I can replace it."

Molly scowled at him. "Excuse me, but aren't you getting a little proprietorial, there? If anything needs replacing *I'll* replace it, which it doesn't, and

I won't because I'm not staying. Now could we get back to the subject at hand?"

He seemed amused by her outburst. One raven's wing eyebrow lifted slightly, and a spark came into his eyes—which right now were more of an aqua than emerald, a close match to the color of the ocean that she could glimpse over his shoulder. "Sorry if I seemed pushy, that's just the way we do things here. We help one another out. What is the subject?"

A woman of good grace would have been ashamed of herself at that point, and Molly did have to admit to a tiny twinge. But she was first and foremost a reporter with a question, and if she had not allowed his see-through pants to distract her, she certainly was not going to be waylaid by her own conscience.

"The subject," she said firmly, "is the painting."

He arranged his features into an expression of polite interest. "What about it?"

"Who painted it, for one thing?"

He glanced again toward the fireplace. "Isn't there a signature?"

Molly banged one crutch against the floor in frustration, almost overbalancing herself. He made a quick move toward her but she recovered herself and accused him, "You know perfectly well there's a signature! It's *your* signature! Now—" she drew a calming breath "—let's go through this one more time. You—or someone who looks remarkably like you—are featured in a one-hundred-year-old painting that just happens to be hanging over my fireplace. Your signature is also on that painting. Now, I think we have to agree that you couldn't possibly have painted that picture, or even modeled for it a hundred years ago. So—"

Her eyes narrowed as they moved over him. It was a shame, really. All the good ones were either criminals or con men. "The only possible conclusion I can reach is that Sean Seaward is not your real name. It was just the only thing you could think of last night on the spur of the moment. And I don't think it was any coincidence you just happened to be on the beach steps last night. You knew I was coming, you said so yourself, and you were waiting for me. I think you have a very specific interest in that painting—maybe you want to buy it, maybe you want to steal it—and that's why you showed up here this morning, checking out my window locks and how sharp my knives are."

"So that's what you do for a living!" he exclaimed. "You write mysteries!"

"I write the *news*," she informed him, scowling fiercely. "And I've written enough of it to know a scam when I see one."

His gaze was patient and amused, not in the least insulted. And after a moment of respectful silence, he said, "There is another explanation, you know."

"Oh, yeah? Well I can't wait to hear it."

He surveyed the area until he saw what he was looking for—the book Molly had been carrying when she answered the door, the one with his portrait on the cover. He walked over to the table and picked it up. "It could be," he said, flipping through the book, "that the painting was done by an ancestor of mine who had a penchant for self-portraits. It could be that there is a strong family resemblance, and for that reason I was named for him."

He brought the book to her, open to a page at the back. The short article featured a bad black-and-white photograph of a man in a starched collar and wide tie whose oddly streaked hair was pulled back at the nape. The caption read, About The Cover Artist.

Sean added, "It could even be that my ancestor once owned this cottage."

She looked at him, startled, then quickly scanned the article. Sean Seaward, a native of Harbor Island during the late nineteenth century, produced a number of fantasy paintings of the sea before his mysterious disappearance in 1895. *The Sea King* is his most famous work.

Molly limped over to the sofa and sat down, still holding the book—mostly because it gave her an excuse not to look at him while she tried to think of a way to apologize. She *hated* admitting she was wrong. Particularly when she wasn't entirely convinced.

The whole thing was just so terribly neat, she thought. A look-alike ancestor. An egotistical artist who used himself for a model. And if this cottage had once belonged to Sean's family, that would certainly explain his interest in it, even his apparent familiarity with it. It would also explain why a painting depicting a man who resembled him was hanging over the fireplace. In fact, in a few simple sentences, he had explained everything, and *that* was what bothered her.

When she couldn't postpone it any longer, she released a puff of breath, twisted her mouth wryly and looked up at him. "Well, I guess you'll have to forgive me. I've had a really rough summer."

"So it would appear." He nodded at her cast. "How did you hurt your foot?"

"I was chasing down a story," she said, and explained. "I guess I must have been getting on my editor's nerves," she added, "because he insisted I take time off—and sent me here." She looked around meaningfully. "Obviously, he's very creative when it comes to punishment."

Sean grinned. "It's a long way from shipshape, that's for certain. And you're in no condition to do much about it."

"Even if I wanted to spend my vacation cleaning someone else's house," she returned pithily, "which I don't." She set the book aside. "Listen, it was good of you to come by, and whatever you're cooking smells really great, but I'm going to have to get on the road if I don't want to end up sleeping in my car tonight. It's hard to find a motel that will take dogs, you know—especially once they get a look at Delilah."

"She's a fine dog."

"She's a brontosaurus."

Molly reached for her crutches and struggled to get to her feet. He leaned down to help her, his hand fastening on her arm in firm support. His nearness went through her with a thrill of pleasure and a taste of the sea, sun washed and drowsy bright. His eyes really were the most incredible shade of aqua.

She caught herself hesitating a moment too long, gazing a little too raptly, and was embarrassed. A subtle sparkle in his eyes told her he had noticed, too, and that annoyed her. She took her crutches in one hand and allowed him to help her to her feet, pulling away from his touch as soon as she was standing.

"Where *is* that dog, anyway?" she muttered, looking out toward the porch, which was now empty.

There was no mistaking the appreciative sweep of his gaze over her figure as she turned away, and it made her skin tingle. When she moved toward the porch, calling for Delilah, she could feel his eyes following her, making her heart beat a little faster, forming a pleasant knot of heat at the back of her neck. The man had a definite, indefinable sex appeal, much like a low-voltage magnetic field. You couldn't see it, you couldn't smell it, but a woman, once having stumbled into its influence, could definitely feel it.

And it wasn't as though Molly was easily impressed. She had dated prize-fighters, race-car drivers and foreign correspondents. She knew sex appeal, and this was definitely it. She couldn't help wondering if it was that, more than any other single factor, that made her so suspicious of him.

Molly had not had the best luck in her relationships with men. Not surprising, considering her bulldoglike determination to find something wrong with each and every one of them. Perhaps she had reached a point where she was disqualifying them simply because they were male. She hoped not, for if so, she *really* owed Seaward—or whatever his name might be—an apology. Not to mention what an unfortunate attitude like that could do to her already-Spartan sex life.

To get her mind off that train of thought, she went to the porch and called loudly for Delilah. There was no response. She rattled the food dishes, calling again, "Delilah!"

"She's probably gone down to the beach to chase sea gulls," suggested Sean behind her.

"She never wanders off. Wouldn't you just know, the one day I don't have time to chase her down..."

She turned and went back through the house, which was the fastest way to reach the sea side of the building. She pushed open the glass door and stepped outside into the wash of brilliant sunshine and the taste of the sea. The sounds of the ocean mixed with the tumble and tug of contrary breezes, sea grasses waved and gulls dipped and soared against a cobalt blue sky.

"Wow," she said, breathing deeply of the salty air. "I guess I can see why a dog wouldn't want to come inside on a day like this. This is beautiful, isn't it?"

"Humans shouldn't be inside on a day like this, either," he said. "Didn't you come to the sea for your health? I suggest you take advantage of it."

She laughed, trying to restore with her fingers the part the wind had made in her hair. "I don't know how much good the sea can do for a broken ankle. But I've got to admit this is nice."

"Let's walk down, then."

"Well, maybe to the top of the stairs. We might be able to see Delilah on the beach."

He gestured her to precede him.

Molly took up her crutches and proceeded down the boardwalk. "You know," she said conversationally, "that story about your ancestor is really pretty good. But I don't see how that house could be a hundred years old."

"Parts of it are even older."

She cast him a skeptical glance over her shoulder.

"Oh, yes," he assured her, coming up beside her. "A great many houses on the island are. You'll find that's true of many places where materials are hard to come by and it's cheaper to make do than do over."

"Oh, come on. It's hardly that isolated. The only thing that even makes this place an island is a thirty-foot bridge over a swamp."

"River," he corrected. "A river which regularly floods, I might add. And you must remember the bridge is a fairly recent addition."

She snorted. "It's fifty years old if it's a day."

He smiled. "As I said, a recent addition."

"All right, then, John. I have another question for you."

"What's that?"

"Aha!" She pivoted toward him, lifting one crutch for emphasis and almost whacking him with it in the process. He stepped aside just in time to avert disaster, she placed both crutches firmly on the ground and accused, "I knew it!"

His expression was patently baffled. "Knew what?"

"That Sean Seaward wasn't your name. You just answered to John!"

He lifted an eyebrow. "I was trying to be polite. John is the Anglicization of the Irish Sean, isn't it?"

She stared at him for a long moment, trying to think of an appropriate argument. Finally, she turned and started down the boardwalk again. "You have an answer for everything, don't you?"

"Not everything."

There was a note of something wistful in his voice that made Molly wish she could see his face. But he had fallen a step behind her and she didn't dare try another quick maneuver with her crutches.

A moment later, she said, "So, you're Irish."

"No."

"But you said—"

"I believe I said the name was Irish."

"Do you practice this?"

"Practice what?"

"Being enigmatic."

"Is that what I'm being?"

She swung around, forgetting caution in her frustration. "You know perfectly well—"

He ducked quickly, catching the crutch just before it caught him broadside on the shoulder. Molly wobbled to balance herself, chagrined, as he looked at her. His expression was dry.

"If you can cause this much trouble on crutches," he said, "I'd hate to know what you were like before you broke your foot."

"Ankle," she mumbled, tugging to retrieve her crutch. "I broke my ankle."

"I think," Sean said, taking the crutch from her grip, "it might be safer for all concerned if I held on to this."

She glared at him, struggling to maintain her balance. "What am I supposed to hold on to?"

"How about me?"

He slipped his arm around her waist, offering her his support on her uninjured side while she used the remaining crutch to support the side with the cast. A little hesitantly, Molly slipped her arm around him, bracing her hand against his back. She was not known for her grace of movement, and she had her doubts about being able to accomplish this—no matter how pleasant the prospect.

"This might take a little practice," she warned him.

He smiled. "I'm a patient man."

But to her very great surprise, walking with him was easy. With grace, he effortlessly matched his rhythm to hers. Since the accident, she had cursed her helplessness; now she began to see that being dependent on others had definite advantages.

The wind billowed his open shirt, exposing tantalizing views of his smooth golden chest and taut waist. And she couldn't deny that there was something appealing in having a man's arm around her waist, in having his strong shoulder to lean on. It was not very often that she had the opportunity to lean on a man, not very often that she wanted to.

They reached the top of the stairs and Molly caught her breath at the vista that spread below her. The late-morning sun had captured the carpet of crushed shell and broken rock left by the tide and turned the beach into a sheet of gold. Beyond it the sea glittered in shades of blue and green rarely seen outside the Mediterranean, capped by the gentle curl of snowy white surf as it tumbled toward the sand.

"My goodness," Molly said, awed by the beauty. "Will you look at that? It doesn't even look like the Atlantic."

"We had a squall right before you arrived," Sean said. "That often cleans the waters."

"The only seashore storms I've ever seen turned the surf to sludge and left the beaches looking like war zones."

"Well, now, it all depends on what kind of a mood old Trident is in, now, doesn't it?"

She glanced at him and he grinned.

"Trident?" he explained, putting the hint of a question on the word so that it sounded more like a gentle reminder. "Poseidon? Neptune? King of the Sea?"

"Oh, him," she said with an easy familiarity she did not feel.

He chuckled. "I take it you're not much of a seaman—or woman."

She glanced up at him through partially lowered lashes. "And if you couldn't tell that at first glance,

I'd have to say you're not much of a man—or I really *am* losing my touch."

He smiled, eyes crinkling in the sun. "If you really have doubts about that," he said, "perhaps it's I who should worry about losing my touch."

The wind lifted his hair away from his face and lowered it again, parting it with rippling fingers that made Molly wonder what it would feel like beneath hers. His arm was strong around her waist, and without realizing it, she had settled comfortably back against him, his fingers curved into the indentation of her waist in a carefree natural way that was nonetheless provocative—perhaps because it felt so natural. And when she looked into eyes that were as brilliant and as captivating as the glint of sun upon the water, she was dazzled by the sudden intense male-female awareness between them.

"I don't think either one of us has much to worry about, actually," she murmured.

Her throat felt tight and there was a little catch in her breath. She had to force herself to look away from him, clearing her throat before she spoke again. "I, um, don't see Delilah."

"Perhaps she's hiding."

"Why would she do something like that?"

"To keep you from leaving?"

"Hardly. She hated this place last night. She wouldn't even get out of the car."

"Ah, but that was before she met me."

"She hated you, too," Molly reminded him.

"She hadn't given me a chance to work my charms. I've been told I have a way with women."

Molly looked up at him, unable to resist any longer. "I can believe that," she said.

The wind tugged at her curls, blowing strands across her face. With his fingers, he smoothed them back and said, "Why don't you stay, Molly?"

His eyes were alluring, his face so close she could see nothing else. She wanted to see nothing else. The way his hair lifted and fell in the wind, the play of light and shadow across the planes of his face, those eyes.... *Enchanted.* There was no other word for the way she felt.

And she was, after all, on vacation.

"Well," she conceded after a moment, "maybe I will stay for lunch."

He smiled, and she smiled, and they turned back toward the beach. In another moment, as if out of nowhere, Delilah came trotting into view, her tail waving like a banner, leaving wet paw prints in the sand.

Chapter Three

"So," Molly said, settling down at the kitchen table while he dished up big stoneware bowls of the savory-smelling stew. "What is this business about the Sea King?"

She had spent most of the remaining morning watching him toss sticks on the beach for Delilah to chase, basking in the sun and admiring the simple beauty of the male form. Occasionally, he would run into the surf, and the dog, barking with all the playful enthusiasm of a puppy, would follow him in up to her chin—Delilah, who regarded all major bodies of water with the same disdain as did her mistress and who practically had to be tranquilized for a bath. Sean was right. He definitely had a way with females—of the canine variety, at least.

When they'd returned to the house, he insisted on "swabbing down the galley," as he called it, and Molly didn't protest overly much. Even by her standards of hygiene the kitchen was no fit place to serve a meal. But by the time he called her to lunch, the windows were sparkling, the porcelain was white again and several layers of grime had been removed from the linoleum. She sat down at the freshly scrubbed butcher's table with a copy of *Myths and Legends of Coastal New England* in her hand, feeling pampered and spoiled.

I could get used to this, she thought wryly.

He set a bowl of stew before her. "Don't you know about the Sea King? I thought you'd read the story."

"I haven't gotten to it yet." She picked up her spoon and inhaled deeply. "This smells fantastic."

"There's a baker in town—or at least there used to be—who makes incredible brown loaves. I'll go in tomorrow and pick some up."

"Town? There's a town?"

He sat down beside her at the long table with his own soup bowl in hand. "It's more a village, really. It's only a mile or so away, easy walking distance...if, of course, one can walk." He grinned at her as he lifted his spoon.

"I have a car," she reminded him. A town. That put a whole new light on things. Maybe she wouldn't mind being stuck out here in a run-down shack in the middle of nowhere if there was a town only a mile away.

"Is that where you live?" she asked innocently. "In town?"

"No," he replied, and extended his hand. "May I see the book?"

Molly handed it to him, a little annoyed by his refusal to elaborate. But the annoyance evaporated into pure appreciation as she tasted the stew. "This," she told him, "is fantastic."

He took a bite as he flipped through the pages. "Yes," he agreed. "Here it is." He found the page he was looking for and glanced at her. "Shall I read it to you?"

Molly nodded, her mouth full.

"The legend of the Sea King," he read, "is found all over the world and countless versions of the story have been told. Many of the fables have their roots in Greek mythology...and so on and so on...."

He broke from the text and turned the page, scanning for the pertinent section. "Ah, here it is." He began reading again. "One of the most obscure versions comes from an isolated village off the coast of New England called Harbor Island, and reportedly inspired the painting depicted on the cover of this book." He glanced up and added, "That's us."

Molly lifted an eyebrow to show she was properly impressed, but she did not stop eating. She had a few vices; gluttony was one of them.

He resumed reading. "Parents have been frightening young girls for generations with the legend of the Sea King who once every hundred years is reported to break free of his briny prison and take on human form to search out his perfect mate on land. Having found her, he will mesmerize her with his eyes and drag her back to his kingdom under the sea. Should he fail to find her, however, he will be condemned to return alone to the cold depths of the dark abyss and there remain for another hundred years."

He fell silent, and closed the book with a snap. Molly looked up.

"Is that all?"

There was a faint, preoccupied frown between his eyebrows, and his eyes had taken on a grayish tint, as though the sun had gone behind a cloud. "It's not dark, you know. As deep as a human can swim, there's always some ambient light. And the colors are richer, truer, more luxuriant than anything you could ever see on land."

He dropped his gaze to the painting on the cover of the book and absently traced its outlines with the tips of his fingers. "It's not cold, either," he added. "Or at least cold is a relative term. I don't know why they have to make it sound so unpleasant."

Molly put down her spoon, watching him closely.

He came out of his reverie with a shrug. "Anyway, they've got it all wrong. The truth has nothing to do with mesmerizing or dragging anyone into the sea. The lover of the Sea King must come to him willingly and stay with him happily, for only then can he be free of the fate that condemns him to spend his life beneath the sea. It's not the cold or the dark, you see," he explained to her earnestly, "it's the aloneness. He wants only what anyone would want—not to be alone anymore. To have someone to love."

Molly swallowed hard, oddly unsettled. "And what about his poor lover? The one who has to spend the rest of her life under the sea?"

"Don't be absurd. No human can live beneath the sea, not even for love. You see how they've got it all wrong, all these years. It's he who wants to be human, don't you see? And the only way he can be is if the woman he loves invites him to stay."

There was an intensity in his troubled eyes that was—well, mesmerizing. Molly felt a chill tingle at the base of her spine.

Her voice was oddly distant and a little strained as she said, "Why do you suppose he's never found anyone, after all these centuries?"

His smile was sad. "But that's the trick, isn't it? Finding the right woman. And you mustn't forget, he works under a handicap."

"What's that?"

"Every hundred years, he has only a season to find the woman fate has decreed to be his perfect mate. When his time is up, he has no choice but to return to the sea."

"Well, yes. That would be a handicap, I suppose."

She had to struggle to free herself from the spell of his tale. Among his many other talents, she realized, he was a compelling storyteller. For a moment there, he'd had her so caught up in the plight of the Sea King, she'd been talking about him as though he was real. She'd almost *thought* of him as real. The whole thing was romantic nonsense of course, and that was the most amazing part of all—it was not the kind of story that generally even appealed to her.

She gave herself a mental shake and then grinned, leaning one elbow on the table as she pointed a finger at him. "You know," she said, "you're good. I mean, you're *really* good. You're the one who should be writing books."

There was a fraction of hesitance, then the small lines between his eyebrows relaxed and a twinkle came into his eyes. He picked up his spoon again. "I can't think what you mean. I read the story out of the book."

"Yeah, but all that other garbage—"

"Garbage?" he raised his eyebrows in an exaggerated gesture of insult. "I'd watch how I speak, if I were you. We're very protective of our heroes around these parts."

"Heroes, ha! What's so heroic about this guy wandering around looking for some poor girl to give him a home? Sounds like a pansy to me."

"Stories of unrequited love are always heroic," he said mildly, finishing off his stew. "Aside from that, it doesn't do to insult the Sea King. If you're not careful, this entire cottage and everything within it could end up as driftwood on some foreign beach."

"Since we're at least a hundred feet above sea level, I rather doubt that."

"Stranger things have happened," he assured her soberly.

She grinned again, leaning back in her chair. "You sound like you really believe this nonsense. I wouldn't have taken you for a superstitious man."

"All men of the sea are superstitious." He picked up their bowls and took them to the sink. "Are you saying you don't believe it?"

She gave a short bark of laughter. "Oh, yeah, right. Some half fish, half human crawls out of the ocean once every hundred years or so, spends a few months putting the move on everything in skirts he comes across and when he doesn't score by the deadline, he slinks back into the tide again, to try again next century. Sure, didn't I see a profile of him in *U.S. News and World Report* last week?"

Sean leaned against the sink, his arms folded across his chest, a lazy spark of amusement in his eye even as he tried to make his expression sorrowful. "Molly, Molly," he said with an air of feigned reproach. "You are a cynical woman. Have you never learned the value in believing what you can't see?"

"Nope," she admitted blithely. She got her crutches in one hand and pushed up from the table. He came to help her. "And I've never bought nonexistent resort property over the phone or had my entire bank account emptied by some slick-talking televangelist, either. And, I'm happy to say, I will *never* be taken in by the old 'go to bed with me or I'll be doomed to spend eternity under the sea' line."

"A century," he corrected, steadying her arm while she balanced herself on her crutches. "Not eternity. And how can you be sure?"

Had any other person tried to assist Molly the way he did, she would have slapped him away or tripped him with her crutch—as she had done on more than one occasion since her accident; she hated hovering. But Sean didn't hover. He was simply there, quiet and competent, doing what needed to be done as though it were second nature to him. And the truth was that his subtle, low-key sexuality set her nerves to humming in such a distracting way that it did not even occur to Molly to object.

To his question she replied dryly, "I am not easily impressed, I assure you."

"I can see that. On the other hand, the Sea King is known to have a way with women."

He was standing to the right and a little behind her; Molly had to tilt her head back to look at him. The movement brought her face very close to his.

He didn't move away and neither did she. "Then why has it taken him so long to find the right woman?"

One corner of his lips dimpled with amusement. "The right woman is often hard to find."

His breath touched her face when he spoke, his scent mingling with the warm fragrant cooking odors in a tantalizing way. Being close to him like that, cozy and near in the kitchen in the middle of the day, was at once both provocative and oddly comforting. It was a peculiar, heady feeling.

"Right," she responded. "I forgot he's so choosy... and has a time limit."

She started to move away but he surprised her by capturing one of her forward-falling curls between two fingers. His expression was easy and relaxed and his tone conversational, a heart-catching contrast to the intimate gesture as he wrapped her hair around his finger, bringing her face slowly, subtly, and by mere fractions of an inch, closer to his.

"He does, however, have certain advantages," he said.

Molly's heart was beating faster. She tried to calm it. "Like what?"

He smiled. "Incredible good looks, insouciant charm, a persuasive manner..."

And a voice that could charm the fish right out of the sea, thought Molly dazedly.

"And, of course, there's the other thing."

Molly's voice was hoarse. He held her captive with one strand of hair wrapped gently around his finger and with the power of his smiling gaze; it might well have been a chain around her neck for all the chance she had of breaking free. "What other thing?" she asked a bit breathlessly.

With the tip of his thumb he lightly stroked her cheek; a feather touch that she felt all the way down her spine. "A woman," he said softly, "once indebted to the Sea King, can refuse him nothing."

Then he smiled, released her curl from his finger with a playful tug and tapped her lightly on the nose. "So, Molly Blake, I'd suggest you be more careful who you allow to save your life in the future."

Again, Molly couldn't help noticing how mesmeric his eyes were, and she wondered if she would be able to refuse him anything... should he ask.

But it was a fleeting weakness, a passing fancy, and she shrugged it off irritably. "Very funny," she said. Then, remembering her manners as he stepped away, she added, "Thanks for lunch. It was great."

"No trouble. Shall I bring the rest of your things in from the car?"

Molly opened her mouth to refuse, because until that moment she really hadn't changed her mind about staying. Delilah's delaying tactic—if that was what it was—had won her lunch, but that was all.

But suddenly, all her objections to the dismal little cottage no longer seemed valid. In fact, it hardly seemed dismal at all. It was quiet, scenic, restful—all the things Hal had promised it would be. And the prospect of a six-week recuperation period spent here no longer seemed like a prison sentence. In fact, it could be . . . interesting.

And so, before she was even aware of having made a conscious decision, she heard her voice replying, "Sure. Why not?"

It didn't occur to her until later that she had just discovered exactly how hard it was to refuse him whatever he asked.

"DO YOU THINK it would be possible to find a woman in town to come out and do some cleaning?" Molly asked later that afternoon.

"No."

Sean set the last carton—a collection of five years' worth of notebooks, photographs and clippings that she intended to turn into a book—on the floor beside her desk. She had cleared the big rolltop of its miscellany and was setting up her PC, connecting cables and wires. Sean watched with interest.

"Why not?"

"You can't get anyone from town to come out here. They think the place is haunted."

Molly paused and slanted him a skeptical look. Her tone was flat. "What?"

"Haunted may not be the right word," he conceded. "More like troubled. At any rate, you won't get anyone to come in, not this time of year."

We'll see about that, Molly thought, resolving at that moment to drive into town the first thing in the morning. She regarded him thoughtfully. "You really work hard at making these things up, don't you?"

He grinned. "It's not easy, keeping a lady like you interested."

Her pulse quickened a beat or two, though she tried to sound casual. "Interested in what?"

In him? If that was what he was worried about, she could put his mind at ease right then, because she was *very* interested. But on second thought, perhaps it wouldn't be wise to tell him so.

He replied with a twinkle, "Just interested." Then, "You're right, though. You're going to need someone to help you make this place livable."

"What I need," she said, turning back to her work, "is a telephone. I'll call Hal, tell him in no uncertain terms what I think of his sending me to this dump and make *him* send someone out to clean it up."

"Hal would be—"

"The owner."

Sean nodded. "He should have taken better care of the place," he agreed. "But until he can get someone out here, why don't I help you get it back into shape? Fix the loose shingles, straighten up that porch, and the front step has almost rotted through. The railings need tightening and the doors are warped—"

"Whoa there!" Molly held up a hand in protest. "I just needed somebody to clear out a few cobwebs. You're talking major renovations."

"You can't have the roof leaking all over your fancy electronic equipment," he explained. "And if that front step collapses, you're likely to break your other ankle. You can't stay here by yourself with doors that won't close and window handles that are broken. But don't worry, we'll get the cobwebs cleaned out, too."

She frowned a little. "We?"

He replied cheerfully, "Oh course. You can't expect to appreciate this place until you've put a little sweat into it."

"I don't want to appreciate it. I just want clean sheets and hot water—and a bathtub that won't grow mushrooms."

He chuckled. "We'll have it shipshape in no time."

Molly hesitated. She would be crazy to accept his offer. He was a perfect stranger who had insinuated himself into her house and yes, her confidence, far too smoothly. Everything about him was suspicious and he seemed to enjoy her suspicions. He stood before the open window, looking like an old-world poet in his open white shirt and wavy hair, smiling down at her in a way that made her feel no sensible woman would even consider sending him away...even when she knew very well there was nothing sensible at all about allowing him to stay.

"It's nice of you to offer," she said, "but I couldn't accept. I mean, don't you have a job?"

"I can spare the time."

She watched him carefully. "What is it you do, exactly?"

"Don't worry, I'm perfectly capable of wielding a hammer."

Molly tried, not very successfully, to hide her frustration. "That's *not* what I asked."

"Would you like me to move the desk in front of the window for you? You can enjoy the view and the sea breeze while you work."

But she refused to be distracted. "I asked," she repeated firmly, "what it is you do for a living?"

The small line that appeared between his eyebrows was puzzled and amused. "Why do you want to know?"

Molly opened her mouth to reply and was surprised to find no good answer came readily to her lips. There were many answers, of course—curiosity, reassurance, curiosity, references, driving curiosity—but it was a moment before she found one that was suitable.

"Because—because—" she stammered. "Well, because I just do, that's all. Because I have to know how much to pay you, and if you make more than

I do, it would be an insult to offer to pay you at all, now, wouldn't it?"

He laughed softly. "I have no need of your money, Molly Blake. So, if that's the only problem, accept my help in the spirit it was offered—as a neighborly welcome to the island."

Molly suspected he knew very well that was not the only problem, and she doubted whether even island neighborliness would extend to such an investment of time in a vacationer's home.

Before she could say anything further, however, he cast an assessive gaze over the water-stained ceiling and sagging shelves and added, "And I do feel I have some responsibility. After all, it's my—That is, it was my ancestor's home."

She frowned a little, recognizing the near slip but unable to fathom what it meant. In fact, she couldn't figure out anything about Sean Seaward, his motives or his intentions, and that, she knew, was the primary reason she could not even consider refusing his offer. Well, she had to admit as she watched the tightening of his arm muscles as he stretched to test the strength of a baluster several risers up the staircase, maybe it was the second reason.

And if she were perfectly honest with herself, she knew that if Sean Seaward had walked out of her life this afternoon, she would have found a way to bring him back. Never in her life had she been able to resist a mystery, particularly if there was a hint of danger attached. And Sean Seaward was a custom fit to that description.

She regarded him speculatively. "Well, if you're certain it wouldn't be an imposition..."

"I'm certain."

"It might be kind of interesting to have you around, at that."

He smiled, the sparkle in his eyes reminding her of a glint of sunlight on a wave. "Oh, it will be interesting," he said. "I can promise you that."

"YOU WERE IN the navy, right?" Molly observed sourly five hours later.

She was grimy, sweaty and exhausted; she didn't think she'd ever get the odor of chlorine bleach and pine cleaner out of her hair or the grunge from beneath her fingernails. But the transformation in the little cottage was remarkable.

Sean returned from emptying what was perhaps the fifteenth pail of dirty water. His whites, she was grimly pleased to see, were water splotched and smudged, in little better shape than her own clothes.

"What makes you say that?"

"Don't try to deny it. Every navy man I've ever known has been obsessed with cleanliness, and you're the worst of the lot."

He had actually suggested scrubbing the joints between the baseboards and the floor with a toothbrush—an idea that Molly vetoed right away.

He grinned. "I guess you could say I know my way around the sea."

He paused in the middle of the living room and cast a critical eye around. "It's starting to look better."

As far as Molly was concerned, it was perfect. The bathroom and kitchen sparkled; she had had nothing to do with those two rooms. Layers of dust had been lifted from the living room, the windows had been washed, the front porch swept. Linens had been airing in the sun all afternoon and a freshly made, outdoors-scented bed awaited her in the cozy sleeping loft. Of course, there were still tons of books, magazines and miscellaneous junk to be sorted through and neatened and she could tell by the look on Sean's face that none of the end results of all of Molly's hard work quite met his standards. But she was finished. She didn't work this hard on her own apartment and she lived there—more or less—twelve months out of the year.

"It looks great," she said. "Better than great. You could perform surgery in here. Hal wouldn't recognize the place. And I've had it."

She was sitting on the floor, legs stretched out before her, drying silverware—or tin ware, actually. Delilah was stretched out beside her, watching lazily as Molly plucked the last fork from the bowl of soapy water, dried it and tossed it onto the tray of clean items.

"You think too much, Molly," Sean told her, coming over to her with his hands extended. "A little physical labor is exactly what you need—it gives you a chance to use your other muscles."

Molly grasped his hands to pull herself up. "You forget I'm recovering from a serious injury."

"How could I? You reminded me every time I put a sponge in your hand."

Standing was still tricky business, and Molly was halfway to her feet when she lost her balance. His arm came quickly around her waist to steady her.

"You see?" she challenged, bracing her hand against his chest. "I'm definitely handicapped."

He smiled, and with a gesture that was too natural to be a caress but too tender to be anything else, he smoothed an errant curl away from her forehead. "I think," he said, "it would take more than a broken ankle to handicap you, Molly Blake."

She felt again that peculiar tightening of her throat that his nearness caused, the slight quickening of her pulse. It would have been so easy to slide her fingers across the smooth warm muscles of his chest, to curve her hands around his neck, to lift her face to his.... And what would he do if she did? For a moment, caught in the soft blues and greens of his gaze, she thought she knew.

And then he handed her the crutches and stepped away. "You're sure you're going to be able to get up the stairs by yourself?" he said. "It would be no trouble to bring the bed down here."

"It would be a lot of trouble. But the world is full of stairs and I have another month on crutches."

"True enough. There's plenty of stew left from lunch, and you know how to reheat it."

She made a wry face at his questioning look. "I know how."

"Do you need anything else?"

"A good bottle of wine would be nice."

"I'll see what I can do." He smiled and touched a finger to his forehead in salute, starting toward the door. "Meanwhile, I'd better be on my way."

She swung around toward him. "You're leaving?"

"I'll be back tomorrow," he assured her.

"I mean—you're not staying for dinner? You cooked it, after all."

"Enjoy it." He opened the door.

Molly was strangely disappointed. All afternoon, she'd looked forward to dinner with him, watching the sunset with him....

Before he could leave she said quickly, "Can I give you a ride?"

"It's not far."

"Where do you live?"

"That way." He gestured toward the back windows, which could have indicated anything from the mainland to China. "Really, it's not far. I'll see you tomorrow."

She couldn't think of any other way to detain him. "Right. And thanks!" she called after him as he shut the door behind him. He waved to her through the glass and started down the boardwalk.

"He probably has to hurry home to the wife and kids," she grumbled, threading her fingers through Delilah's coarse fur.

She would have given anything to know where he lived, but short of getting in her car and following him—which might have been a little obvious, all things considered—it didn't look as though she'd be finding out tonight. And then something occurred to her.

Moving as quickly as she dared, Molly maneuvered up the stairs. It was a slow and arduous climb and by the time she reached the floor-to-ceiling window in the sleeping loft, she was breathing hard.

The vista spread out before her was breathtaking. The sharp precipice on which the house was situated gave way to a smooth expanse of peach-colored beach, frothed by surf and marked at its far north end by a border of broken boulders. Beyond it the sea was a dozen or more shades of blue, ranging from azure to deepest midnight, the whole sparked by golden glints of the setting sun. Molly propped one hand against the window frame and just stood there, drawing in the beauty, and she understood how some people could spend an entire vacation gazing out over the sea.

She was disappointed, though, that her vantage point offered no view of a road or path or even a nearby chimney top in the direction Sean had indicated. In fact, there was nothing to give a hint as to where he might have gone. And then, just as she was about to turn away, he came into view on the beach below her.

She watched as he stepped out of his shoes and shrugged off his shirt, stowing both in the crevice of a boulder, safe against the wind. The sun gave a golden cast to his sculpted shoulders and leanly defined biceps, the breeze lifted his hair and shadowed his profile. Molly caught her breath as he unfastened his pants and stepped out of them, stuffing them behind the rock with the rest of his garments. Thrusting his fingers through his hair as though to free his thoughts in the same way he had just unfettered his body, he walked naked into the surf.

His body was truly a beautiful thing to watch. The flare of shoulders from slim waist, tight buttocks, strong thighs, sinewy calves. There were no visible tan lines; his skin was that same delicate golden color all over, and Molly couldn't help marveling over that. His movements were supple and graceful, almost liquid. Even on land he moved like a swimmer.

He walked until the surf splashed over his waist and then, with the next big wave, he sliced neatly into the water with a grace and economy of movement that reminded Molly of a diving dolphin. The sheer and simple beauty of it caused her chest to tighten with pleasure.

It was a long time before he surfaced again, and Molly began to grow anxious. She stepped closer to the window, searching the undulating waves for a sign of his figure. When she caught sight of him again, it was almost by accident, for he swam in such perfect rhythm with the sea he seemed almost a part of it, like a sun shadow or a fish. His strokes were strong and easy and barely rippled the surface of the water; his wavy hair streamed out behind him. He flipped in the water and floated, he dived and surfaced again, he let the tide carry him. Molly smiled as she watched him, pleased to see how much delight he took from the water.

She kept expecting him to turn around and start for shore; to dress and begin his journey home, wherever that might be. But he didn't. He kept swimming, long, easy strokes that led him straight out to sea. Molly's smile faded as he grew smaller and smaller in the distance. She watched until a protruding finger of land obscured him from view and still she watched, expecting to see him reappear, swimming toward shore, any moment. She waited, pressed against the glass, searching the darkening ocean until her eyes hurt, but he never returned.

By the time she turned away from the window, she was no longer smiling. Her features were, in fact, drawn into a troubled frown.

This Sean Seaward was growing into more of a mystery with every moment. She was beginning to wonder whether agreeing to stay had really been such a wise decision, after all.

Chapter Four

The next morning Molly charged Delilah with guarding the cottage, and she drove in the general direction in which Sean had indicated the village lay. She was somewhat surprised to actually find it, a little over a mile away.

It wasn't much of a village, to be sure. There was a worn marina with a fishing dock and a tackle shop, a post office with a faded flag and one small block of ramshackle clapboard buildings that served, apparently, as the business and shopping district. Molly went first to the pay phone at the edge of a deserted-looking service station and dialed the paper with her calling card.

"Very funny, Hal," she said when he finally came on the line. "I'm still laughing. I'm in stitches."

"Molly!" His voice was too boisterous. "Good to hear from you! Having a good time?"

"I'm having a great time. I just love sleeping with spiders and taking cold showers in rusty water and scraping three layers of dust off of every dish before I eat on it."

"What's wrong?" He sounded innocent. "No hot water?"

"Hot water is the least of your problems," she retorted, for, in fact, Sean had gotten the water heater working fine before he left yesterday. "As far as I'm concerned, you've got plenty of it. For God's sake, Hal, if you wanted to punish me, why didn't you just send me to Siberia like any other halfway imaginative boss would have done? Do you have any idea how long it's been since anyone even *looked* at this cottage of yours?"

"Oh, I don't know," he answered vaguely, "it's been a while. Betty and I bought it right after we were married. . . ."

Molly groaned. Hal and Betty had just celebrated their thirty-fifth wedding anniversary. "And you haven't been back since?"

"Well, hell, it's not as though it's just around the corner, now, is it, Molly? I bought it as an investment, not as a primary residence."

Molly said dryly, "Uh-huh."

She was beginning to put the picture together. Betty was one of the most fastidious people Molly knew. She had no doubt taken one look at the place thirty-five years ago and had refused to set foot in it until it was renovated. Hal, too lazy to fix it up, had just let it slide, hoping it would increase in value until he got ready to sell.

"Well, I'm sorry if it's not up to your standards, Princess Grace," he was saying. "Shall I send a coach and four to fetch you home?"

"You might have at least mentioned that it's not exactly handicap-accessible. I am on crutches, remember? Just how am I supposed to climb down a hundred or so stairs to the beach? Not to mention the loft where my bed is?"

"Oh." For a moment, he actually sounded chagrined. "I forgot about that."

"Obviously. Let me ask you this. All that junk—the books and magazines and paintings and stuff—where did you get it?"

"It came with the house," he answered. "It was an estate sale, fully furnished."

"Whose estate?"

"Hell, Molly, you expect me to remember that? It was thirty-five years ago!"

"And you're a newspaperman. Was the name..." And here she felt herself tense expectantly, hesitating over the name. "Seaward?"

He thought about it only a moment. "No, nothing like that. Roberts, Robinson, Robson—Robins, that was it. Samuel Robins."

For some reason, Molly was disappointed. She felt her shoulders sag like sails suddenly deprived of wind. "You're sure?"

"Of course, I'm sure. Why do you ask?"

"No reason." She twisted one curl around her finger, a nervous habit that only afflicted her when she was unsure. Now she remembered Sean's finger wrapped around her curl in the same way yesterday, and she quickly stopped.

"You don't mind if I go through the papers and stuff I find there, then?" she asked.

"Mind? Hell, why should I mind? More to the point, why should you—" He broke off with a stifled groan. "Good God, I should have known. What are you trying to dig up now? You can't really think you've got a story way out there. Don't you even know the meaning of the word 'vacation'?"

"Who said anything about a story?" She tried not to sound too defensive. "All I want to do is clear out a path to the front door!"

"Let me explain it to you. Vacation—a period of rest from regular work or activity, commonly used for recreation and relaxation. And what happened to that book you were going to write, anyway?"

"Oh, like you really care if I spend my vacation working on another prizewinning story for you instead of a boxful of memories for myself. For your information, hotshot, this town just happens to be crawling with Nazi war criminals and *I'm* taking the story to our biggest competitor!"

"Town?" Hal said. "There's a town there?"

Molly released an exasperated breath. "Goodbye, Hal. Thanks for all your support."

She hung up the phone and made her way back to her car. Once inside, she waved at the pair of eyes she was sure had been watching her from behind the crusty windows of the service station.

Her next stop proved more fruitful. During the course of her career as an investigative reporter, Molly had seen the inside of her share of barrooms, poolrooms and dark private clubs. The general store in the center of the downtown shopping district was something of a departure from her usual environs, but it didn't take her long to feel at home. She was once again tracking down a mystery and she had come to the right place.

On the outside, the paint was flaking and the porch was leaning—common around these parts—and the faded sign over the screen door said, Ritter's Gen'l Merchandise. Inside, the store was dark and warm, and crowded with every conceivable item from dusty swimming floats to hamburger meat.

The man behind the counter nodded to her when she came in and watched as she clumped over to the stack of wire shopping baskets beside the magazine racks—magazines, Molly couldn't help noticing, that were all a month or more out of date.

"Need some help there, young lady?"

Molly looked in dismay from the tangle of wire baskets to her crutches. Some things, she was beginning to see, were impossible to do by herself. "Well, actually..."

He came from around the counter, a small, bald man with friendly brown eyes. "Why don't you just give me your list and let me gather up your goods. Have a seat over there by the window."

"I don't really have a list," Molly explained, wishing she'd thought of it. "I just got in a couple of days ago and—"

"Oh, sure." He nodded as though just recalling a piece of vital information. "You're the one that moved into Gull Cottage. Staying long?"

"A month or so. How fresh is the shrimp?"

"Fresh frozen. You want fresher, I'd recommend the haddock."

"No, that's fine. I'll take a pound."

He went toward the cooler at the back and Molly sank onto the long bench in front of the window. "Have you been here long?" she inquired conversationally.

"Since six this morning."

Molly hid a grin. "I meant the store—in this location."

"Since 1879," he replied without missing a beat. He returned to the counter with a package wrapped in white butcher's paper and added, deadpan, "Of course, I didn't start in until 1948. What else for you now?"

"Bread, cheddar cheese, milk, margarine—I don't suppose you have a nice white wine, do you?"

"How about beer?"

"Fine."

She watched as he moved around the store, collecting items with leisurely efficiency. "So you've been here quite a while," she commented. "I guess you know all there is to know about the history of Gull Cottage."

"Not much to know. It's stood vacant most that I can remember. How're you planning to fix these shrimp?"

"Um, boil them, I guess."

He looked disapproving and tossed a small jar of cocktail sauce into the basket.

"What I meant about the cottage was, I was told it was pretty old."

"Oh, right enough. Quite a landmark around these parts. 'Course, we've got more than one of those, too."

"What do you mean?"

"Well, there's the old lighthouse—"

"No, I mean about my house being a landmark. Somebody," she added casually, "told me it was haunted."

He gave a dry little chuckle. "Haunted, is it? I wouldn't be surprised. You're not in the market to buy the place, now, are you?"

It was her turn to laugh. "Hardly. My boss owns the place, it's just on loan."

"Nice boss."

"Depends on how you look at it."

His eyes twinkled when he glanced at her. "I can see what you mean. Like I say, the place has pretty much stood empty since old Sam passed on."

"Sam?"

"Robins. He used to own the place. Anyway, you don't go paying any mind to that talk about it being haunted. There's not a building on this island that's not tied up with one local legend or another." He set a basket on the counter that was a lot fuller than she had expected. "I got you some green and yellow vegetables, some salt and pepper, other things you might need."

"Potato chips?"

He went for them.

"What kind of legends?" She raised her voice a little to follow him.

"That place? Seems it's mostly tied up with that Sea King story."

Molly's heartbeat stuttered.

"What—uh, what story is that?"

"Just something the fishermen banter about. Can't say as I rightly recall all the pieces of it."

He brought the potato chips to the basket and leaned both forearms on the counter thoughtfully. "Seems to me it has something to do with a sailor that took on a curse and had to live underwater...yeah, that's it, more or less. But now that you bring it up, I can't for the life of me think how any of it ties in with Gull Cottage."

He shrugged, cleared his forehead and smiled at her. "Now, what else?"

With great difficulty, Molly made her own expression neutral and her smile pleasant. She reached into her pocket and pulled out the broken window handle. "Do you have anything to replace this?"

"I'm sure we can find something."

He found the new window handle along with a veritable treasure trove of taco mixes and canned chow mein. Molly took some of each, added ice cream and cookies and paid the total.

As he was boxing up the groceries, she asked, "Do you know anybody around here named Seaward?"

"Can't say as I do. This time of year, there're not but fifty or sixty families on the island, and I know 'em all. You might check with Leon down at the marina, though—could be somebody hired on to one of the boats."

Molly's throat was tight with disappointment. "Thanks, I'll do that."

"He's not there now, of course. Catch him this evening, or before sunup, when the boats are in."

Strike three, she thought.

He carried the boxes out to her car. "Name's Ritter, by the way. I own the store."

Molly introduced herself.

"How in this world are you managing up there all by yourself?" he asked. "I mean, on crutches and all. Do you have any help?"

Molly hesitated. When she spoke, the words surprised her. "Actually, I do." She was referring to Sean. Sean Seaward who as far as she could discover didn't even exist, and if he *did* exist, might be anything from a con artist to a mass murderer. Yet he had offered to help her fix up the place and she had accepted and she had every expectation that he would keep his bargain.

It was crazy.

She added, as the last of the boxes was loaded, "I could use a telephone, though. Where do I go to see about having one installed?"

He scratched his bald pate. "Well, now, that is a problem. I guess you could drive in to Jefferson, think there's a telephone office there. But it's liable to take six or eight weeks for them to get out here with one. Guess that wouldn't do you much good, huh?"

"Guess not," she agreed, sighing, and got into the car. "Thanks for all your help."

"Anytime, now." He waved as she drove away.

Molly vaguely considered spending the rest of the day exploring the countryside—perhaps finding a little café where she could while away the afternoon baking in the sun and watching the surf roll in—and, along the way, satisfy her curiosity about what lay in the direction in which Sean had swum.

First she'd put away the groceries and pick up Delilah, and, if her timing was right, she'd turn back toward town when Leon was due back at the marina.

But something else occurred to her. The proprietor of the store had referred to the boats coming in late in the afternoon. How then had Sean obtained fresh seafood early yesterday morning?

When she pulled up in front of the house, Delilah came bounding up to meet her, causing a frown of consternation to cross Molly's face. She'd left the dog securely locked inside.

"Delilah!" she scolded as she opened the car door. "How did you get out? Did you break a window? You know you're supposed to stay put when I'm not home!"

As she struggled to get her crutches out the door, a firm hand suddenly appeared to assist her.

"Sorry," a male voice said. "She sounded so pitiful locked up in there, I thought I'd let her out for a run. I didn't know she had orders to the contrary."

Molly let her gaze move slowly upward from a pair of sandaled feet, over strong, golden tanned legs, across a pair of masculine thighs and frayed denim shorts, a faded red T-shirt, upward to a strong chin, wavy dark hair and morning-sea eyes. Sean Seaward smiled down at her. Why was she surprised?

Why was she *not* surprised?

She accepted his extended hand to pull herself upright. "That pitiful act of hers is well rehearsed," she said. "Sorry she pulled it on you."

"My fault. I always was a sucker for a female in distress."

His smile was contagious. Molly returned it, however uneasily.

And she had to ask. "How did you get in?"

"Do you mean, how did I let the dog out?"

She nodded.

"The back door locks don't work. Of course, not many people around here worry about locking their doors, but better safe than sorry, I guess. I'll start on them right after I finish bracing up the front steps."

Over his shoulder Molly could see a sawhorse, various sizes of lumber and several tools scattered around. It all looked very industrious.

He was serious. He really was volunteering his time to fix up the cottage for her.

He really had come back.

Molly got situated on her crutches and moved to the back of the car, opening the hatchback. "I went into town today."

"So I see." He picked up a box of groceries.

"If you'd given me a list, I could have picked up what you needed."

"No problem. I'll take care of it as I go along." He put a second box under his other arm.

"I did get the handles for the windows."

"Good."

"Mr. Ritter at the store had never heard of you."

He was halfway up the driveway, with Molly trailing behind on her crutches. He stopped and gave her an amused look. "Checking up on me?"

She couldn't believe she had blurted it out like that. She had spent years perfecting a technique that was so subtle the subject didn't even know he was being interviewed until she nailed him. Now it was as though she had forgotten everything she had ever learned, ever *invented.* What was happening to her?

Yet she maintained her cool. With a very deliberate effort, she looked him in the eye and replied, "Is there any reason I shouldn't?"

He laughed and stepped up onto the porch. "None at all. Let me put these boxes down and I'll help you up."

He had completely removed the step that led to the porch, and he was right—getting up without it was a tricky maneuver on crutches. Molly did it, anyway, and succeeded more from luck than skill.

The look he gave her when he turned and found her right behind him was amused and admiring. Molly also thought she saw a certain knowledge in his eyes of exactly what her maneuver had meant—she wouldn't be indebted to a man she was about to interrogate, even if that debt was for no more than assistance with a high step.

"Why do you think he had never heard of you?"

"Is there any reason he should have?" he replied.

"He said he knew everyone on the island."

"Obviously he doesn't."

"How long have you been here, anyway?"

"Not long. I think you have ice cream melting. Do you need any help putting those things away?"

"Look," she said impatiently. "I don't mean to pry, but—"

"And I don't mean to cut you off," he said, looking out the window, "but I see your dog is walking off with my hammer. Hey!" he called, and whistled sharply. "Delilah!"

He whistled again and was out the back door before Molly could say another word.

For a moment, she scowled irritably, but then she caught sight of him, playfully tugging the hammer from Delilah's mouth, and she couldn't help smiling. Maybe it was just her imagination. Maybe there was nothing mysterious about him at all. Maybe he really wasn't avoiding her questions. And if he was, what did that prove? Nothing except that he was an ordinary citizen who did not have to tolerate her attempts to invade his privacy... particularly since he had done nothing but go out of his way to accommodate her from the beginning.

And perhaps that was what bothered Molly the most. She simply wasn't used to people being nice to her for no reason; she was always trying to track down the motive. In the case of Sean Seaward, the utter lack of an ulterior motive was the most confusing thing of all.

Chapter Five

The sound of hammering and sawing provided an oddly soothing background to the remainder of Molly's day. She knew there was no reason for her not to proceed with her original plan and explore her surroundings, but the purpose behind her explorations made her feel guilty somehow. The man was working up a sweat on her behalf for free; to continue to investigate him behind his back felt like a betrayal.

Besides, the whole thing was silly. She didn't initiate a full-scale background check on every laborer she hired—most of the time, she didn't even check their references—so why should Sean Seaward be any different?

There was an answer to that, but it was too complex for Molly to examine at that time.

She thought she might work on her book a little, and got as far as dragging the box of collected clippings over to the desk before one of the dusty volumes stacked on the end table distracted her. It was a history of sailing ships with a long section on mysterious disappearances, and Molly found it fascinating.

When her stomach began to growl, she went to the kitchen and mixed up a bowl of tuna salad for sandwiches. She called out the window to Sean, asking him if he wanted to join her.

He had taken off his shirt, and tied back his hair with a red bandanna. His shoulders and chest glistened with sweat, muscles flexing as he executed a final thrust of the saw into the wood and a neat section of two-by-four fell to the ground.

He straightened up and blotted his forehead with the back of his arm, squinting in the sun as he turned toward the window. "Thanks," he called back, "but I think I'll take a dip instead."

"You've got to eat something," she protested, and winced at how maternal that sounded. "I mean, what about replacing all those calories you're burning off?"

He grinned. "I had a big breakfast. I'll take you up on an early dinner if you're interested, though."

"I'm boiling shrimp."

"Perfect. I found a nice white wine for you last night."

"Where? The man at the store looked at me as though I was trying to buy illegal drugs when I asked for some wine this morning."

He gave a negligent lift of his shoulders. "I had it lying around. I'd almost forgotten about it."

"Well, if you're bringing the wine, you're definitely invited."

He saluted her with a touch of his fingers to his forehead. "Deal."

She watched him saunter down the boardwalk toward the beach, Delilah trotting in his shadow. He had a great walk, she decided. Tight buttocks, even stride, good calves. Even his ankles were attractive, long-tendoned and strong. He wore denim shorts as though it was a look designed exclusively for him. Watching him, Molly couldn't suppress a small sigh of simple pleasure.

She resisted the urge to climb upstairs and watch him undress for the swim. There was a fine line between admiration and voyeurism.

BY SUNSET, the cottage possessed a new set of front steps and a porch that did not sag. The back-door locks were repaired and the front door no longer stuck. A rebuilt gate hung perfectly suspended from the new hinges, and the window handles had been replaced. All in all, not a bad day's work, and Molly was as pleased as though she had accomplished it all herself.

"It's amazing how much vicarious pleasure you can get from watching someone else work himself to death," she told Sean when he returned to the house from his after-work dip in the ocean.

He chuckled. "I'm in no danger of that, but I'm glad you enjoyed it."

His hair was wet and shiny, his skin even a deeper gold after a day of working in the sun. The sparkle in his eyes was relaxed and amused, and seemed to suggest he knew *exactly* what she had enjoyed most about watching him work.

Molly turned quickly back to the stove, where a pot of boiling water held the shrimp while the oven heated garlic bread. She was wearing a pair of cotton drawstring shorts, with one leg slit up the side almost to the panty line to accommodate her cast, and a soft gray T-shirt with an etching of a cigar-smoking cat on the front. The humidity in the kitchen was high, causing her curls to stick to the sheen of perspiration on her forehead, and forming damp spots on her T-shirt between her breasts. She could feel Sean's eyes focused on those spots of dampness, the curve of flesh around them.

"I made a salad," she said, "but I don't know how good it will be. Mr. Ritter didn't have a big selection of fresh vegetables."

"It's a little past season up here. Here, let me do that."

He moved forward as she took up the slotted spoon to remove the shrimp. His arm brushed against hers with a pleasant tingle of flesh-to-flesh contact—brief, warm, oddly tantalizing. She handed over the spoon and stepped aside, fluffing her limp curls with her fingers in a self-conscious gesture.

"Why don't we make a picnic outside?" he said. "There's a basket on top of the cabinet over there that I think is big enough."

"Good idea."

Molly spotted the basket, surveyed the situation and plotted her strategy. She positioned herself beside the cabinet, lifted her crutch and hooked the basket, neatly lowering it to the floor.

Sean laughed when he saw her maneuver. "You like doing things for yourself, don't you?"

She shrugged. "I don't know whether I like it particularly. But I'm used to it."

"Why is that?"

She took the salad out of the refrigerator while he drained the shrimp. "Why is what?"

"Why are you used to doing things for yourself?"

"I don't know. It comes with the territory, I guess." She put plates, napkins and silverware into the basket. "I've been alone most of my life."

"You're an orphan?"

Molly hesitated. "No." She waited until he brought the bowl of shrimp over to the basket and then she added, holding his gaze, "My mother lives in Tucson with some guy I've never met. My father is in prison."

He showed absolutely no reaction. He simply looked at her for a moment longer, then he said,

"Do you have a blanket you don't mind getting sand on?"

Molly decided right then that she liked him. A lot.

"There's one on the back of the sofa, I think. I'll get the garlic bread out of the oven."

He carried the basket and the blanket down the boardwalk with Molly only a few steps behind and Delilah glued to his side, her eyes fixed upon the picnic basket. A warm sea breeze tousled Molly's hair and sent little spouts of sand scurrying before them while the sky faded into gentle shades of pastel.

Sean looked back at her when he reached the top of the stairs. "Shall we go down?"

Molly drew up beside him, looking down over the panorama of deep green water and pale pink sand with longing. "What a stupid idea," she said, annoyed with herself. "To come all the way to the ocean and then not even be able to go to the beach. Even if I could get down the stairs," she explained, "I'd be sure to get sand in the cast, and wouldn't *that* be fun. So I guess I stay here."

"No problem." He spread the blanket on the sand beside the boardwalk. "How long until the cast comes off?"

"Three weeks, if I'm lucky. But I won't be completely off the crutches for six."

"That's not so long."

"Too long for me."

His smile was vacant, his expression thoughtful as he murmured, "Six weeks. The season will be half-over."

She looked at him curiously. "What season?"

And he came back to himself with a smile. "Autumn, of course. Winter always comes too soon, doesn't it?"

Molly dropped one crutch to the ground and used the other to lower herself to the blanket. Sean moved forward, taking her arm to steady her. "On a day like today, nothing could be further away."

She breathed deeply of the salt-scented air, exhaling in a long slow sigh as she looked down over the ocean. The water was the color of some exotic jewel, the surf lay like a scallop of frothy lace on the shore. "I didn't think the ocean *got* that color around here," she said wonderingly.

"They say it means the Sea King is in a good mood."

Molly frowned. *Him again.*

She opened her mouth to query him, but he didn't give her a chance. "I left the wine cooling in a tidal pool. I'll be right back."

Delilah bounded down the steps with him, and Molly watched until they both disappeared around a bluff and she could not tell where they went.

"Damn this cast, anyway," she muttered.

She hated being left behind. She hated to sit and wait. Now, of course, she had no choice but to accept both in good grace.

Molly was never very good at being idle, however, and while he was gone she couldn't help speculating, letting the familiar questions and curiosities turn over in her head. Where did he live, what did he do? Where had he come from, what did he want? Who *was* he?

He returned less than ten minutes later with a dark green wine bottle in his hand and the sea breeze ruffling his hair. He came up the steps with all the grace of an athlete, and Molly couldn't help but admire the sight of him. A fine net of sand clung to his lower legs and feet, and when he sat beside her, leaning back on his heels, she noticed the hem of his shorts was wet. She also noticed the leanness of his thighs, their firm masculine shape and definition, and the pattern of dark, gold-tinted hair that covered them.

"You could have put the wine in my refrigerator, you know."

"It's better this way." He had taken most of the steps at a run, but he was barely winded. He reached into the basket for a corkscrew.

"I'll bet you were a professional swimmer."

He found the corkscrew and glanced at her with a twinkle in his eye. "What makes you think that?"

"Who else would go swimming in the dark and the fog and in seas as rough as they were the night we met? Besides, you're in great shape. You're obviously an athlete of some sort."

"Thank you." He worked the cork free of the bottle and scooped up the two glasses Molly had set out.

She nibbled at a shrimp, watching him. "Well, are you?"

"What?"

"A swimmer."

"I never miss a chance."

That was not exactly the answer she had been waiting for, but she would have sounded foolish had she pursued the subject. She accepted the glass he offered and took a sip.

A small moan of surprised pleasure escaped her and she held the glass out to the light, admiring its clarity and glow. "That," she declared sincerely, "is the best thing I have ever put in my mouth. What is it?"

He picked up the bottle, turning it around. "Sorry. The label must have fallen off in the water."

She took the bottle from him. There was no paper label but a small metal tag was suspended from a chain around the neck. It had been stamped with a place and date, and Molly squinted to read it. "Château..." The next word was almost completely worn away. "Something, France. Nineteen..." She turned the tag to the light to make sure there was no mistake. "Thirty-six? Nineteen thirty-six?" She stared at him. "Are you telling me I'm drinking a pre-World War II wine?"

"So it would appear."

"A wine that's older than I am?"

He grinned. "I think that's safe to say."

Molly put the bottle back into the basket almost reverently, and regarded her glass with new respect. "No wonder it tastes so good."

He smiled. "Glad you like it. May I make a toast?"

Molly quickly swallowed her second sip and said, "Of course."

He held up his glass, and she did the same. His gaze, smiling and lovely, held her captive. And he said simply, "To our season. May it be everything we both have waited for."

Molly hardly knew how to respond to that. In fact, she didn't respond at all—she didn't even know what to think—and when he touched his glass to hers, she quickly lowered her eyes before taking a sip, embarrassed and confused.

There was a moment or two of awkward silence. Sean served his plate, and so did Molly. Delilah came by, looked at each of them hopefully in turn, then gave up and trotted down toward the beach.

Molly broke off a crust of garlic bread.

"So," she said, trying to ease into her line of questioning, "the cottage has been in your family a long time."

"Not really."

"I thought you said your ancestor built it. I just assumed your family had owned it until modern times."

He speared a forkful of salad. "I'm sure I didn't say that."

Molly tried to repress her frustration. "I guess I misunderstood. I just got the impression that all the work you're doing was more of a labor of love than anything else."

"It is."

There was something in the quiet, matter-of-fact way he said that, in the steadiness of his crystal gaze, that made Molly's heart skip a beat, and left her more confused than ever.

"What's out there?" she inquired, gesturing toward the northeast.

He looked over his shoulder in the direction she indicated, then back at her. His eyes squinted a little in the dying sunlight, forming fine-webbed lines at the corners of his eyes. The breeze parted his hair, then smoothed it again, then tossed it in random careless patterns. Molly experienced a moment of sheer wonder that she was actually having dinner with a man like this, and not just dinner but a picnic on the beach.

And what was she doing? Interrogating him, of course.

He suggested, "The sea?"

Molly frowned. "No, I mean beyond that."

He popped a shrimp into his mouth, chewing thoughtfully. "Nova Scotia?"

"I saw you swimming last night."

His expression relaxed. He picked up his wineglass. "You do enjoy that, don't you?"

"That's beside the point."

"I didn't know there was a point."

"The point is, you looked as though you were going somewhere. I just wondered where, that's all."

"I was going somewhere." He lifted his glass to her with a grin. "For a swim."

She said sourly, "You really do enjoy being mysterious, don't you?"

"No, but you do."

"What on earth are you talking about?"

"Having a puzzle to put together, a mystery to solve, a story to chase down—you're never happier than when in the middle of something you'd probably be better off leaving alone. I knew that the first minute I met you."

She tried to frown. "That's ridiculous. How could you possibly know such a thing?"

"There's only one kind of woman who would try to descend an unfamiliar, hundred-foot set of stairs in the dark, on crutches, in the fog." He sipped his wine. "Intrepid."

Molly struggled to hold back a grin. "Maybe. And maybe I'm just intrepid enough to find out the truth about you."

Sunlight caught in his eyes, giving them a cellophane sheen. "Maybe you are. Or maybe you should just relax and let me entertain you. After all, you're supposed to be on vacation."

Molly bit into a shrimp, feeling relaxed and oddly flirtatious. "Oh, yeah? How would you entertain me?"

He shifted his position slightly, to look out over the ocean, and for a moment he didn't respond. And then he said, "Look." He lifted his hand, pointing toward the sea.

Molly saw Delilah, sniffing the sand and leaping out of the way when the surf came too close to her paws. She saw gulls diving for their dinner and fat little seabirds mincing across the beach.

Sean moved close to her, slipping a hand around her neck, guiding her head toward the direction in which he gazed. Molly's heart started to beat faster.

"There," he said. "Out to sea. Do you see it?"

She saw what appeared to be a large floating shadow just beneath the surface of the water, and she gasped as that shadow took shape and partially broke the surface. A geyser of water erupted into the air and she cried, "A whale!"

She looked excitedly at Sean, then back to the ocean. "My God, I've never seen one before, not in person! I didn't know there were whales around here this time of year! Aren't they usually farther north?"

"Usually," he agreed. His hand tightened fractionally on the back of her neck. "Look. His wife."

Another shape appeared at a distance, grew closer, then broke the surface with its sleek shiny back near its mate. Molly watched the shapes and shadows move in a graceful, playful dance—surfacing, diving, swimming, circling. She was in awe.

"They mate for life, you know," Sean said. "I've known a whale to grieve himself to death when his mate dies unexpectedly."

She turned slowly to look at him. His face was very close to hers, his eyes deep enough to drown in. Her breath caught as his fingertips caressed the back of her neck, sending a shiver down her spine. The intent in his eyes was gentle and clear, and her pulse raced to read it. She didn't want to avoid it, she ached with anticipation for it. Yet...

"You're a sailor, aren't you?" Her voice was breathless, a little hoarse. "Or a fisherman. You have a boat anchored offshore somewhere, and that's where you live. That's why no one has ever heard of you. That's how you were able to bring me fresh seafood before the boats come in. Isn't it?"

He smiled. His fingers spread over the side of her face, leisurely and warm, threading into the short hair behind her ear. "Is it?"

Molly tried to swallow, but her throat was too dry. Her pulse was racing. "Why won't you answer me?"

"Why do you want to know?"

"Because," she said. His fingertips slid down her throat, and where he touched, electric pulses of pleasure throbbed. It was hard to concentrate. "Because I think you're going to kiss me and I'd like to know who you are first."

He smiled. She could feel herself floating away on that smile, carried off by the sea of his eyes.

"But wouldn't it be fun, just once, to be kissed by a stranger?" he asked softly.

His breath infused her, dizzying, intoxicating, flooding her veins with heat. His lips touched hers, as soft as a whisper, as sure as the beat of her heart. It was a kiss like no other she had ever known. He tasted of hot wet nights and old wine and the sea. Her senses reeled with the impact of him. Every pore of her skin opened to him, was filled with him. There was nothing else in her world but him. She could feel a part of herself start to open and flow toward him, even as a part of him seemed to be seeping, as though by osmosis, into her. There had never been a moment of purer, all-encompassing pleasure in her life, and as long as she was in his arms, captured in his spell, she did not want anything else.

It was like being in one of those sensory-deprivation chambers, where all time, all meaning, all sensation on the physical plane ceased...only in reverse. It was like being captured in a bubble filled with light and sound. It was like being under the influence of some powerful drug through which everything else was filtered out except sensation. It was like being transported, by a method she could not imagine to a place she had never guessed existed, a place of feeling, of emotion, of sheer, unblemished sensuality.

When the kiss was over, the loss of him was almost painful. Separating from him left her stunned, aching, at a complete loss. He was food and drink to her, he was the air she breathed, he was the blood in her veins...and all from a single kiss. His hands had not moved, nor had hers. He had done that to her with a kiss.

She opened her eyes, and almost expected night to have fallen. Aeons had passed in his arms, and only seconds. Sensibility was a long time returning.

Finally, she managed to say, very hoarsely, "Who are you?"

He smiled, threading his fingers through her hair in a tender stroke. She turned her face to the caress as instinctively as a cat seeking its master's touch. She could feel her heart pounding.

"Haven't you guessed yet?" he said softly. "I am the Sea King, come to take you back with me. Will you come?"

In that moment, she believed him. With no effort at all, she could have said yes, would have promised him anything. She had asked who he was; now she began to realize she no longer knew who she was.

It was that thought, more than anything else, that brought her back to herself. Still, all she could manage was, "I—um, I can't swim. I'm afraid of the water."

He smiled. "That does create a problem, doesn't it?" He moved a little away and picked up his wineglass again. "In that case, perhaps we'd better finish dinner."

Molly nodded and turned back to her plate. She didn't taste anything else she ate. She couldn't stop looking at Sean.

She knew how it felt to have fallen under a spell.

Chapter Six

"Incredible."

It was 6:00 a.m., and Molly had been watching the spectacle since the first rays of sun had begun to splash the waves with golden color. Delilah, who had first awakened her by scratching to go out, was racing up and down the beach, barking happily. Molly, observing it all from her loft window, understood how she felt. It was a beautiful thing to see.

Just beyond the breakers, a school of dolphins played with all the carefree abandon of kindergartners at recess. They jumped, they flipped, they twirled in the water and chased one another in circles. And in the midst of them, swimming as gracefully as though he belonged to them, was Sean.

He dived and came up with something in his hand—for not the first time in the past week, Molly longed for a pair of binoculars—which he threw out into the ocean. One of the dolphins went after it like a puppy chasing a stick, while two others, swimming in almost perfect unison, trailed him. A fourth suddenly surfaced right in front of Sean, a huge, magnificent creature. Laughing, Sean put his arms around the animal's neck and let it lift him out of the water.

Molly's hand went to her throat. The resemblance between the scene being played out before her and the one depicted on the canvas over the fireplace was uncanny. She had to turn away from the window for a moment, shaking away the cobwebs.

"I have *got* to get out more," she murmured out loud. "I'm going to go batty."

Over the past week, Molly had discovered isolation for the first time in her life. There was no television, no radio, no telephone. For all she knew, natural disasters might have destroyed major metropolitan centers, global war might have been declared and the wearing of hats proclaimed a felony. She had no contact with the outside world whatsoever—except for Sean. And he did not seem like a contact from the outside world at all; if anything, he was a world unto himself. Yet because of him, she didn't miss anything else.

For thirty years, Molly had been in the center of things, either causing trouble or enjoying it, stirring things up or cheering others on while they did. She could not recall a single period in her life when she had done absolutely nothing. And never in her wildest dreams had she imagined enjoying it.

She knew that such indolence, such isolation couldn't possibly be good for her; she knew she should be going stir-crazy by now. Instead, she actually felt calmer, more stress-free, than she had in years. And looking back over the past week, she couldn't name a single thing that she had accomplished.

Her days began late, with soft bands of sunshine slanting over her bed and the sound of hammering outside, or early, like this, with the sight of Sean walking from the water after his morning swim, naked and beautiful. It ended as she watched him swim away into the indigo sea. In between, the hours were azure and sun splashed, filled with lazy meanderings through dusty books on arcane subjects, and colored with the sound of his voice, the flash of his smile, the warmth of his eyes.

He told her impossible stories of the sea peopled with fantastic creatures and treasure caves and bold, dashing sailors, and laughed when she demanded to know where the tales had come from. But as easily as he could weave these odysseys, he could reel off equally fascinating facts about marine life—some so improbable she accused him of making them up, but were authentic, nonetheless.

Once he saw her reading a book on shell identification and the next morning brought her a basket of shells to catalog. It was a silly pastime and one Molly had never thought she would enjoy but she spent an entire day matching shells to their pictures in the book. What would her hard-bitten colleagues at the paper think if they could see her now?

She was falling into the rhythms of this place, the rise and swell of tides, the lap of the surf, the phases of the moon . . . its eccentricities, its enchantments, its legends. After a week such as this, was it any wonder that she could gaze at a perfectly real, thoroughly contemporary, maddeningly mysterious man and think of legends that were hundreds of years old?

As though drawn by a power greater than her will, Molly turned back to the window. Sean was walking out of the surf, wet hair clinging to his neck and scalp, shoulders glistening with a sheen of saltwater. The flat plane of his abdomen, strong thighs, the dark shadow of his sex. . . . The longing that stabbed through Molly was as sharp as hunger, and just as insistent.

Delilah bounded beside him and he tangled his hand in the dog's fur, speaking to her playfully. Then he stopped, and looked up toward the house. Though she knew it was impossible, Molly could have sworn he could see her from there, standing at the window. He seemed to look right at her.

Molly quickly sank into the shadows, out of his line of sight, lest she be caught spying. Then, on impulse, she turned and scrambled through her drawers for shorts and a T-shirt. Dressing quickly, she made her way downstairs and out to the boardwalk.

As she hoped, he was still there, playing on the beach with Delilah. He had put on a pair of faded, body-molding jeans with the cuffs rolled up to his calves, but no shirt. His hair, drying in the sun, glinted with blue highlights as he ran backward on the beach, calling a playful Delilah to him. The wind carried the sound of his laughter to her and it caught in her chest with a prickle of wonder. Watching him was like watching a poem unfold before her eyes.

She started cautiously down the steps toward the beach.

Delilah noticed her first, when Molly was about midway down the steps, and came bounding toward her with all the dangerous enthusiasm of any one-hundred-thirty-pound child. Molly froze, picturing herself being bowled over by the playful paws of her best friend, and then Sean called Delilah back to him. To Molly's utter astonishment, Delilah obeyed.

Sean raised his arms to Molly in an all-clear signal and Molly proceeded carefully down the remainder of the steps. Sean met her at the bottom, grinning.

"Well," he said. "Fancy meeting you here."

"I thought it was about time I saw for myself what you find so fascinating about this place."

"Well, then allow me to show you."

Without further warning, he swept her off her feet and into his arms. Molly gasped and flung her arms around his neck. "You know I hate it when you do that."

The sparkle in his eyes told her something about her voice must have been less than convincing. It was little wonder. When she was in his arms her will seemed to melt away; she forgot how much she resented being dependent and how much she hated being out of control and remembered only how wonderful it felt to be held by him.

Her lips twisted ruefully. "All right," she admitted. "So maybe there are worse ways to see the beach."

"The beach?" he returned, grinning. "That's not even the best part."

He swung around and started carrying her toward the surf liner.

Molly stiffened a little in his arms, pulling back to look around. She tried to keep her voice light. "I don't think I'm ready to go swimming yet."

"One step at a time," he assured her.

"Come on, Sean, I'm serious. I can't get this cast wet."

"You won't."

Anxiety tightened in her stomach as she looked over his shoulder and saw nothing but greenish blue water and foam-specked waves. Delilah splashed in the tide line beside them, splattering Sean's lower legs with wet sand.

"Isn't the water cold?" she said uneasily.

"It's perfect. Like bathwater."

Foam washed over his ankles, followed almost immediately by a breaker that splashed against his lower legs, wetting the knees of his rolled-up jeans. Molly's arms tightened around his neck convulsively. "All right, that was fun," she said as steadily as she could manage. "Now take me back."

"You wanted to see what I found so fascinating about the beach." His voice was gentle and persuasive and so, when she looked at him, were his eyes. "This is it. Let me share it with you, Molly."

For one brief, intense moment she wished more than anything that he could, that she could let him, that she could let go and experience, just this once, the wonder and majesty of something larger than herself. She looked into those sea-washed eyes and she wanted to go where he went, to know what he knew, to be a part of what he loved.

But then another wave surged, and he waded into it. It broke high on his legs, soaking his jeans, and Molly thought she felt his footing waver with the shifting sand. Sean laughed with delight but Molly smothered a cry in his shoulder.

"All right," she said sharply. "That's enough. Take me back."

But he hardly seemed to hear her. His voice was filled with pleasure, his eyes were snapping with it.

She could feel the rhythms of the sea surging through his muscles, his blood, his skin. It was exhilarating—and frightening.

"Can't you feel it, Molly?" he demanded. "The power, the majesty, the magnificence of it! Can't you feel it?"

But another breaker roared toward them, and she didn't even bother pretending anymore. As Sean shifted her weight in his arms to protect her from the worst of the splash she dug her fingernails into his shoulders and shouted, "Take me back! Damn it, this isn't funny! I told you, I can't swim!"

Even she could hear the note of hysteria in her voice and when he looked at her the laughter in his eyes faded into gentle concern. "Molly, we're in less than three feet of water. And I'm not going to let you fall. Don't you trust me?"

She was far too frightened to dwell upon the significance of that question. She clutched his shoulders as though her life depended upon it—which, in her mind at that moment, it did—and demanded in a low, shaky voice, "Take me back. *Take me back.*"

"All right." He held her closer as he turned into the tide, his voice low and soothing. "It's okay. I will. Don't worry."

She squeezed her eyes tightly shut and buried her face in his shoulder until she heard his splashing steps leave the water. Only then did her heart slow its pounding.

She was embarrassed as he set her gently on the dry sand and retrieved her crutches. She tried to hide it by casually running her fingers through her hair, but when she noticed her hands were still shaking her embarrassment only increased.

"Look," she said, "I'm sorry if I made a big deal. I told you, I'm afraid of the water."

He smiled. "We'll just have to work on that, won't we?"

She examined him carefully but saw no sign of contempt or amusement. He really was a special man.

She glanced uneasily toward the ocean, and then back at him. "It's silly, I know. There's no real reason for it. I've just always been afraid."

He caught a wind-tossed strand of her hair, held it affectionately for a moment and released it. "Everyone's allowed one little weakness. Since you don't seem to have any others, you're entitled."

"Gee, thanks." But inside she was aglow with gratitude. He made everything so easy.

Delilah came loping up, stopped to shake her wet fur all over Molly, then ran up the steps, pausing at the top to look back expectantly. "I guess she wants her breakfast," Molly said, brushing at the water spots on her shorts. "I'd better go feed her before she helps herself."

"Need any help getting up the steps?"

"Thanks. I'm fine."

"Molly."

She looked back.

"I wouldn't have let you fall."

She hesitated, then met his eyes, and tried to smile. She turned away again quickly.

She felt his protective gaze following her until she was safe at the top of the steps.

NO MATTER HOW she tried for the rest of the morning, she couldn't stay focused long enough to make progress with her papers. Something was distracting her mind. Or someone. Sean.

Late in the afternoon, she gave up the fight. "I'm going into town!" she called at the back door. "Do you need anything?"

She was a little embarrassed by how domestic that sounded, but he didn't seem to notice. He came around the corner with a two-by-four balanced on his shoulder, shirtless, hair tied back, sheened with sweat. "Not a thing," he answered, flashing her a smile. "Are you sure you can manage by yourself?"

"Of course." Her tone sounded a little irritated, and to make up for it, she added, "Listen, are you sure I can't pay you for all the supplies you've been using? The lumber, the shingles..."

"Not necessary," he replied, "since I didn't pay for them. The materials all came from that shed out back. I guess your friend must have bought them years ago and never got around to using them."

"Oh," Molly said. That sounded like something Hal would do. "I guess so."

He started to move on and she said quickly, "What are you working on?"

She knew it was unkind to keep him standing in the sun with the heavy piece of lumber, and the minute he looked back at her, she regretted having stopped him. But since the night of the picnic, they had not spent more than a few moments together nor exchanged anything other than a couple of sentences of the most routine conversation. She liked being with him and she acted instinctively to keep him there for a moment longer.

"It's a surprise," he said. "Ask me when you get back."

"Sounds intriguing. Do you want to have dinner with me?"

"Depends on what you're having."

There was a mischievous glint in his eye and she acknowledged it with a faint frown of pretended annoyance. "I'm going to try to find lobster."

"Sounds good. But I'm out of sixty-year-old wine."

"We'll have beer."

He winked at her. "It's a date."

She watched him walk away, smiling, and when he was out of sight, she called for Delilah and the two of them drove into town.

Mr. Ritter greeted her with a smile when she came through the door. "Well now, I figured it was about time you'd be running low on supplies. Emily," he called to a woman in a nearby aisle with a shopping basket over her arm. "This is the girl that's staying up at Gull Cottage. She's thinking about buying the place."

The woman turned and looked her up and down over the tops of her wire-rimmed spectacles. "Are you now?"

"Well, actually—"

But Molly was not allowed to finish her denial. "Lot of work, that old place," the woman went on. "Lot of history, too. You got some help?"

"Yes," Molly said, "as a matter of fact, I do. A man by the name of Sean Seaward." She watched them both carefully for a reaction. "I think he's local. Do either of you know him?"

"Can't say that I do," Emily said, and turned back to her shopping. "You make up your mind whether you're going to stay, now, and we'll give you a nice settling-in party. We can always use fresh blood on the island."

Mr. Ritter paused for a moment to rub his chin, then murmured, "Seaward, Seaward... Seems to me I've heard that name before."

"I mentioned it last time I was in," Molly reminded him.

His face cleared. "That must be it, then. Now, young lady, what can I get for you today?"

Molly placed her order for the staples: a six-pack of beer, dog food and some candles. She thought she might put a cloth on the table tonight, cut some flowers if she could find any and light some candles. She gave herself a mental shake—she *never* did sappy things like that.

Which might be one reason she hadn't had a steady boyfriend in six years.

Not, of course, that she was in the market for one, or if she was, that Sean Seaward would be a possible candidate. The man had no visible means of support, but he could afford museum-quality bottles of wine. He was, as far as Molly could tell, unencumbered by a permanent address. On an island of less than fifty families, no one had ever heard of him. He was obviously either a beach bum, a thief or a liar. At her age, and with her experience in life, she couldn't possibly be attracted to a man like that.

Then why was she planning a candlelight dinner for him? Why did all her best dreams revolve around him and why did she awake with a smile on her face thinking of him? Why was she so fiercely determined to prove to herself that he wasn't—or perhaps that he *was*—her type of man?

"I thought I'd stop by the marina and see what's fresh today," she said as Mr. Ritter carried her purchases out to the car. She had deliberately timed her trip so that the boats would be in and Leon would be on duty.

"They've been making a good haul, lately," he replied, placing her boxes in the back. "Tides are up. You'll want to follow this road out of town and turn left on the shell road. You'll see it."

Delilah stuck her head out the window and he came around to scratch her ears. "Good-looking hound. By the way," he added, "I put a copy of the *Gazette* in with your things—just a little local newspaper telling about our goings-on."

A newspaper? He might as well have said "life preserver" to a drowning man. "Thanks!" she exclaimed.

"Well, I recall you were asking questions last time you were in. I thought you might find some answers in the paper. Just comes out every other week, you know."

Molly thanked him again and got in the car. She was so excited about the newspaper that she was almost tempted to dig it out of the grocery box and read it sitting in her car. She had to remind herself that the only things in life worth doing were worth savoring.

She smelled the marina long before she saw it. If she had expected quaint or picturesque—or even inoffensive—she would have been disappointed. The marina consisted of a gravel parking lot, an engine repair/fuel shed and a rambling, weathered building with faded signs that advertised Boat Rentals, Gear, Bait and Licenses. A murky-looking harbor held a couple of rusty trawlers and a shrimp boat, along with a dozen or so hard-eyed, dirty men in hip boots and slickers.

Inside, the building smelled of old damp wood permanently permeated with the aroma of fish. The only light was from a couple of bare bulbs suspended from the ceiling, and beneath her crutches, the floor creaked like the boards of a ship. She spotted Leon immediately; he was the only one not wearing oilcloth.

"Help you?" he asked, squinting at her suspiciously.

He was a small, skinny man whose squint might have been more myopic than impolite. She decided to give him the benefit of the doubt. "How's the lobster?"

He gestured toward an aquarium where several dozen of the beasts floated and crawled in the water. "Good as you'll find anywhere on the coast."

"Pick me out a couple, will you?" With a shrug of her shoulders, she indicated the crutches. "If I try it, I'll probably knock a hole in the glass with these things."

He grinned, and the ice was broken. While he caught the lobsters—picking out the two plumpest, she noticed—Molly told him who she was, where she was staying, why she was here. They chatted about the island, boats and fishing. One by one, the fishermen wandered in, leaning against the cooler in the back and helping themselves to beers, watching and listening to her. Every once in a while, one of them would throw in a remark. She accepted compliments on her dog, who was really too big to go unnoticed hanging her head out the window of a Honda.

And when she felt she had established a good rapport, she inquired casually, "Listen, any of you guys know anything about a man called Seaward? Sean Seaward?"

Whenever she asked that question, she expected dramatic silence, meaningful looks, suspicious behavior. She was disappointed when Leon scratched his head, pursed his lips and said, "Good-looking young fella? White streak in his hair?"

It was so mundane, after all this anxiety, to find her answers in a bait shop. Nonetheless, her heart speeded excitedly and she replied, "Yes. That's him. You know him?"

Leon shook his head. "Nope. Can't say that I do."

She stared at him.

"He was in here, though, once or twice. Brought me a net— You remember, Jake, the one I sold to you."

Jake, a huge man with a chest-length beard, nodded gravely. "Fine piece of work."

"Every knot hand-tied," added Leon. "Don't see craftsmanship like that anymore."

"So," asked Molly casually, "there's a living in that? Making nets?"

A guffaw went up around the room. "Hell, no," somebody said.

"Wish there was," said another.

"Just something sailors do in their spare time," explained Leon.

"Is that what this Seaward is?" she asked. "A sailor?"

Leon shrugged. "Beats me."

"But if he had a boat, anchored somewhere offshore, you'd know it, wouldn't you?"

"Maybe, maybe not. Now, if it was licensed someplace else—"

"But you'd know about it, wouldn't you?" she insisted, a little desperately. She turned to the room. "I mean, you boys know everything that goes on in these waters."

They seemed to agree with that. Someone said, "Well, you know there was that fancy yacht—"

"Something like that, I don't have nothing to do with," Leon said.

"What yacht?" demanded Molly.

"Well, I can't say as how I remember the registry," admitted the first speaker, "but it surely was a piece of work. Anchored about a mile and a half out, beautiful thing. Must have been, oh, a week or more."

The reporter in Molly celebrated victory. The rush was incredible. Of course. He was some eccentric millionaire, slumming on the island. Who knew why people like that did the things they did? The point was, he could be categorized, pegged, explained....

And then the speaker added, "'Course, that was some time ago."

Molly felt dismay seep through her bones. "You mean the yacht's not there anymore?"

"Not that I know anything about." He glanced around the group. "Any of you boys?"

They shook their heads.

"And Seaward," she insisted, "you'd never met him before he came in with the net? He didn't do any other business with any of you?"

Again, a unanimous negative.

"You looking for him?" inquired Leon, fastening down the lid on her yellow pail of lobster. "'Cause if you are, we could put a message on the board there. Most everybody on the island comes by this way sooner or later."

"Thanks." Molly smiled wanly. "I'll probably see him before you do."

So, that was it. The great investigative reporter, stumped again. Damn, she hated this. There was more than curiosity involved now. Her entire reputation, her image of herself, was at stake. This, she decided grimly as she got in the car, was now a quest.

THE MINUTE the cottage came into view she was struck by the changes. It was the first time she had had a chance to see the house from the outside since Sean had started working on it, and the transformation, though far from miraculous, was definitely an improvement. It looked inviting. Almost charming. All it needed, she decided, was a fresh coat of paint. She'd ask Sean what he thought about painting the front door blue.

Of course, there was an awful lot to be done with the inside. Deep green walls, and dark blue for the built-ins and cabinets. Bleached floors, scrubbed furniture, the colors of the beach. She might even tear out those horrible double doors and odd-size windows and put in an entire glass wall overlooking the ocean....

She caught herself with a muffled, uneasy laugh, making plans as though this were her cottage, as though she planned to stay here. It was ridiculous, of course. She would have to make sure Hal compensated Sean for all the work he had done on the place, but beyond that, none of it was really of any interest to her.

She couldn't help remembering what the fisherman had said about the net. A craftsman, that was what he had called Sean. And it was a word, Molly realized, that described him perfectly. The time he had taken with this place, the careful, exacting work he had done with almost no tools and few materials...yes, a craftsman. That was exactly what he was.

And that made one thing she knew about him.

He came around the corner as she was getting out the car, and carried the groceries inside for her. He had changed from his work clothes into the white cotton pants and shirt in which he looked most delectable, and he smelled as fresh and clean as a sun-washed day. Just being near him made Molly want to slip into something clingy and fluff up her hair and dab perfume between her breasts.

Such impulses embarrassed her.

"I'll put these away for you," he volunteered as they reached the kitchen. "Why don't you go outside and see what I've been working on for the past two days."

Molly seized the opportunity. "Nothing major, I hope," she said, starting for the door. "You know I'm just a guest here."

"Oh, I don't think your boss would mind. See what you think."

Delilah accompanied her outside, leading the way down the boardwalk as though she knew exactly where she was going. Molly had barely rounded the corner when she saw it, and she stopped, catching her breath in surprise.

At the top of the steps leading to the sea, on a flat square of ground to the side of the boardwalk, there was now a gazebo. It was built of weathered wood with a shake-shingle roof and lattice on three sides, and it looked as though it had been there forever. It *belonged* there, as if the original designer of the house had always meant to include a gazebo but had run out of time or money before he could build it. Hal would definitely not mind this improvement.

"How do you like it?"

His voice was so close, it startled her, and when she turned to reply, he startled her again by sweeping her off her feet and into his arms, letting the crutches clatter to the ground.

"My goodness," she gasped, putting her arms around his neck.

He grinned. "Is that a comment on my carpentry skills or my personal charm?"

"Both, I think."

He carried her down the boardwalk. "I thought you might like a place where you can sit and watch the ocean until you're able to go down to the beach," he explained. "It's a shame to come all the way to the shore and spend most of your time shut away from the view."

Inside, the gazebo was furnished with a simple wooden bench that followed the curve of the walls, and a medium-size table that Molly vaguely recognized as one that might have supported a stack of magazines in a corner of the kitchen. Spread before her as far as she could see was a vista of sea and sky and sandy beach.

He lowered her gently to the floor, but Molly did not attempt to move away from him. With her arms still looped around his neck and their torsos still touching at all points, Molly looked up at him seriously and inquired, "Why are you doing all this?"

The gentlest of smiles softened his lips and his eyes deepened with an emotion that made Molly's heart beat harder.

"Haven't you guessed? It's all a part of my grand plan of seduction."

Molly swallowed hard on a sudden thickness in her throat. Still, her voice sounded husky as she replied, "You don't have to work nearly this hard if that's all you want."

His face filled her entire vision, his eyes drew her in. Her heart pounded out a tight, steady rhythm and every beat was like a plea, or a demand: *Kiss me... Yes, kiss me...please...*

And he did. His hands cupped her face, fingers threading into her hair. Heat spread from his touch throughout her body in slow enervating waves, her heartbeat closed up her throat. His face moved closer. She couldn't breathe. She didn't want to.

His lips touched hers, barely a whisper of flesh against flesh. She tasted his breath, his moistness, and ached for more. She strained against him but didn't move. Hardly a touch, barely a promise.

And he whispered into her open mouth, "But it isn't. It isn't all I want."

His tongue swept the inner flesh of her parted lips, sending a shiver of desire through every nerve of Molly's body. His fingers tightened briefly against her head and she thought he would draw her closer, she cried out inside for him to draw her closer, but he did not.

He lifted his face, holding her gaze steady with his. His eyes were dark, his voice low. "And you know that, don't you, Molly?"

His eyes searched hers, probing and demanding with a kind of power that forced an answer from her even if no words were spoken. Yes, she knew. She knew and it terrified her.

He took her arm, and lowered it from his neck. She thought then he was going to push her away. Her heart ached with the possibility.

He took her arm in both hands, turning it up so that the soft inner flesh was exposed to his gaze. He looked at her arm, at that very ordinary part of her body to which she had scarcely paid any attention before, as though he had never seen anything so beautiful before. She could feel his eyes like a caress, feather-whispers, tantalizing the sensitive skin of her arm, inch by inch.

And then, slowly, he lowered his face. Hot, moist breath infused the tender flesh, penetrating her pores, fanning into her blood. And then his mouth, his tongue, his passion pressed into her. Her knees went weak. A gasp escaped her and then she had no more breath. The nerve receptors on her inner elbow were suddenly charged with awareness, hot with desire that spread like a fever across the network of her skin. Suddenly, that delicate area of flesh and muscle was the most erotic spot on her body, because he had touched her there, he had kissed her. She was weak with desire for him.

He lifted his face, holding her with his eyes. The sound of their intermingled breathing was an echo of the distant surf, thunderous, whispering. One hand still caressed her face, her hair. The other moved down, tracing the shape of her hip and her thigh, gathering up the gauzy material of her skirt until his fingers were against smooth naked flesh.

His eyes were alight with a dark hot fire. His fingertips caressed her inner thigh, teasing, promising. His breath seared her face. Molly did not breathe at all. Every fiber of her being was focused on the exquisite strands of desire that were spiraling upward from the touch of his fingers. Anticipation blossomed, ached, threatened to explode.

He whispered again, "Don't you, Molly?"

His hand closed upon her upper thigh, the backs of his fingers brushing her soft cotton panties. Dizziness soared. And then his hand trailed downward and away.

He kissed her lightly on the lips and moved away.

This time, the shiver that went through Molly was shocked and bereft. The absence of him was like a cold crashing wave that caught her unaware. She still burned for him, was breathless with need for him, would have made love with him then and there without another word and he surely knew that... but he had withdrawn.

"How can you do that?" she asked hoarsely. She was still trembling all over, and she tried to hide it.

"How can you just...stop like that? It's not human."

He smiled tenderly, fingers cupping her face once again, lightly threading through her hair. "I thought we'd already established that is one thing I'm not."

"Then..." Still she tried to get her voice under control, talking just to remind herself to breathe. "What are you?"

Long stroking motions smoothed her wind-ruffled hair from her face, his eyes bored their fire into hers. "I am a creature of sea and air and your own desperate imagination," he said softly. "And I've come to take you away from all this."

Looking at him, feeling him, longing for him, she almost could believe it. She could believe he was anyone, anything, that he possessed any power and could work any magic and none of it mattered as long as she could be with him.

"What if I don't want to go?" she asked through lips that were strangely numb.

Slowly, the tension left his touch, the fierceness faded from his expression. He lowered his lashes, shielding the gem-fire enchantment of his eyes from her. "That, of course," he said, "is your choice."

His fingers caressed her face lightly, and left her.

Molly drew a deep, steadying breath and dragged her gaze away from him. Reality spiraled back slowly on a gust of cool sea air. She felt the ground beneath her, heard the ocean far away. *This is crazy. Crazy...*

Molly lowered her arms from around his neck, bracing her hand against a support post as she sank to the bench. Her limbs were still trembling, her heart pounding with residual adrenaline, as though she had just had a narrow escape. And perhaps she had. Hadn't she always known that to surrender herself to this man would involve much more than a physical encounter? She didn't know him. Didn't she even have enough self-control to protect herself from what she knew was dangerous?

She must be losing her mind.

Frantically, she cast about for something to say, trying to regain her equilibrium. She had put a dozen men in their places in the past month alone; asserting her mastery over any situation was second nature to her. Why did Sean Seaward leave her at such a complete loss? Why couldn't she think of a single thing to say that would put their relationship back where she wanted it—with her in charge?

Silence lengthened. Days seemed to pass. At last, the only thing she could offer was inane and totally inappropriate: "This is really too generous of you. The gazebo, I mean. I'm going to insist that Hal pay you for the work you put into it."

With a negligent lift of his shoulders, Sean sat next to her, not too close, but close enough to make Molly's skin tingle with a kind of subliminal awareness.

"Not necessary," he said. "I've been meaning to do it— That is, I enjoy working with my hands. I don't get many chances to."

His near slip and quick correction made Molly's eyes narrow curiously, but she knew pressing him would get her nothing but a frivolous reply. She said, instead, very casually, "No, I suppose you don't." And then, with a quick glance that she also tried to keep casual, she added, "You're a marine biologist or researcher of some kind, aren't you?"

Amusement chased away the last remnant of caution in his eyes. "What makes you think that?"

"I've seen you with the dolphins," she confessed. "And you certainly know a lot about marine life—more than the average man on the street, anyway."

"It's just a hobby."

Once again, she found herself trying to disguise her frustration. "But you are a sailor, right?"

A small line appeared between his eyebrows, mitigating amusement with puzzlement—or perhaps a measure of his own frustration. "Why do you ask?"

"Because I want to know, for pete's sake! Why do you think?"

He looked at her thoughtfully. "Have you ever noticed that whenever I start to get close to you, you push me away with your everlasting interrogations? I wonder if you do that with every man who wants more from you than you're willing to give."

Molly scowled fiercely as an uncomfortable color crept up the back of her neck. "I'd hardly call one simple question an interrogation. And I hate being analyzed."

"I'm not overly fond of it myself. And to answer your one simple question . . . Yes. I used to be a sailor."

She followed up quickly. "But not anymore?"

His face remained implacable, though there was no mistaking the shadow that moved over his eyes, like a cloud across the sun. "No. Not anymore."

As a matter of fact, a cloud *had* passed across the sun, and the sea breeze had more than a touch of chill to it now. Molly shivered and glanced around, wishing for the warmth of passion, or even the camaraderie that had been between them only a short time ago. Was he right? Was she pushing him away with her questions whenever he got too close to her? Or was she just asking what any reasonable woman might expect to know about a man who was rapidly becoming a large part of her life?

No, she was just being sensible. "And now?"

His smile did not quite ring true and the sadness in his eyes was haunting. "Now I am just a man trying to please a woman who seems determined to make his task as difficult as possible."

Against her will, Molly was touched, and confused. "Why would you want to please me?"

He looked at her for a moment as though he hadn't heard her, or didn't understand her question. And then he laughed softly and touched a playful finger to her nose. "Because I want to make you fall madly, hopelessly in love with me, of course."

The sun came out from behind the cloud and glinted on the water below. The breeze seemed warmer. Molly relaxed, and murmured just as playfully, "Be careful what you wish for."

He just smiled, making Molly believe for the first time in her life that it might be possible...that she, Molly Blake, who had never cared measurably about anything beyond herself and her own needs, might actually fall in love. The thought, coming out of nowhere the way it did, flustered and bewildered her.

"Look, I hate to ask," she said, "but you are the one who swept me off my feet, so to speak, and I need my crutches if I'm going to make it back to the kitchen to start dinner."

"Stay," he invited. "Enjoy the view. I'll do it."

Her eyes widened with appreciation. "That sounds like an offer I can't refuse. Are you sure?"

He was already on his feet. "Can I bring you anything? Beer, one of your books?"

"There was a newspaper in one of the grocery sacks," she remembered eagerly. "If it's not too much trouble...."

"Not a bit," he assured her, and started back down the boardwalk.

Molly sighed and drew her one good foot up to rest on the bench, propping her chin on her upraised knee as she looked out over the ocean. It was obvious—she was an emotionally dysfunctional, thoroughly pitiable excuse for a human being. The man had offered her nothing but kindness, had repeatedly made one generous gesture after another, and all she could give him in return were suspicions. He had protected her, provided for her and taken care of her and the only thing he had ever asked from her was his privacy...the one thing that she, for whatever twisted reason, could not find it in her heart to give him.

She was ashamed of herself. She wished she could be a better person. She wanted to abandon whatever it was within her that refused to let her take Sean Seaward at face value...but she couldn't.

A gentle nudge of her elbow caught her attention and she looked around to see Delilah standing beside her, the newspaper in her mouth. Molly laughed out loud in surprise and delight.

"Where did you learn *that?*" she demanded, extracting the slightly soggy newspaper from the dog's mouth. "No, don't bother—I know. Is there nothing you wouldn't do for that man?" And then she sighed again and added, "Not that I don't understand the feeling."

She shook out the newspaper and settled back, scanning the headline . . . once, then twice. Sitting up straight as icy fingers gripped her spine, she read the headline a third time.

Sea King Returns, it said.

Chapter Seven

Molly drove to town again the next day. She was up and dressed and in her car before Sean arrived, for she hadn't slept at all the night before. She was somewhat dismayed to find the general store closed when she parked in front of it. The cardboard clock on the front door indicated the proprietor would arrive at 8:30 a.m.

Molly could not remember the last time she had been anywhere before eight-thirty a.m.

While she waited, she unfolded the newspaper and reread the article that was so familiar she had practically memorized every word.

Sea King Returns

Local fishermen have a ready explanation for the unusual meteorological, astronomical and marine conditions that have graced the shores of Harbor Island recently.

Temperatures have remained in the balmy eighties, sunny skies and mild winds prevail. Water temperatures hover in the high seventies, an absolute rarity for this area in October, and have encouraged a variety of tropical marine life to visit our waters.

Schools of blue whale, which normally migrate much farther north this time of year, have been spotted almost daily, as have pods of bottle-nosed dolphins. The dolphins, much to the delight of local residents, are playful and friendly, accompanying the fishing boats as they leave each morning and performing tricks for watchers on shore.

Fishermen report unusually abundant cod catches, as well as a bounteous supply of haddock, mackerel and herring. Several fishermen have reported pulling in grouper and snapper, normally found in Gulf waters, and more than one net has reportedly been brought up filled with shrimp. "Shrimp!" exclaims Ray Peeks of the Deep Rover. "Can you believe that? About the only thing we ain't pulled out of these waters yet is freshwater salmon, and I wouldn't be a bit surprised to run up on a school of them before it's all over. This is bound to be the biggest haul in a single season since before the war. We're all going to prosper."

The plentiful fishing and bizarre marine conditions coincide with the only blue moon this year, as well as a rare alignment of stars and planets which, according to local legend, only occurs once a century. In other words, the Sea King has returned to spread his bounty on the little island he once called home.

For a community whose two sole industries are tourism and fishing, the Sea King's favor couldn't have come at a better time.

And that was it.

The byline was Anna Christianson, and before this day was over Molly intended to find her. Whether she would then proceed to strangle Ms. Christianson or kiss her feet was still under debate, and Molly's decision changed almost hourly.

When she looked up, Mr. Ritter was unlocking the door of the general store. She folded the newspaper again and struggled out of the car with her crutches.

"'Morning," he greeted her cheerfully, holding the door open for her. "You're up and about mighty early."

"I thought you said you opened at six," replied Molly.

"Why, I do. But 'long about eight or so when the crowd thins out, I go on over to the Blue Anchor for a cup of coffee. What can I get for you this morning?"

"Some information," Molly said without preamble. She snapped open the paper and pointed to the lead article. "Where can I find this woman?"

"By gum, I *knew* there was something I should've told you the other day when you was asking." He slapped the counter for emphasis. "Anna's the one you needed to be talking to all along. She pretty much knows all there is to know about this island and the folks on it, living or dead. Yep, that's it." He looked pleased with himself. "You need to talk to Anna."

Molly insisted as patiently as possible, "And I could find her . . . ?"

His face fell. "Oh. Well now, that might be a problem. You see, the newspaper generally suspends publication in October, and Anna goes to Florida to spend the winter with her mother. You could try calling her, though," he added helpfully. "She might not have left yet."

"Thank you," said Molly sincerely. "I'll do that."

He scribbled out a number on a slip of paper and handed it to her. "Anything else today?"

She felt bad about taking up his time without buying anything, so she picked up a loaf of bread and a dozen eggs that she didn't need, along with a couple of out-of-date magazines. Thanking him, she left with her purchases and drove to the nearest pay phone.

There was no answer at Anna Christianson's residence after twenty rings. With a muttered "Damn!" Molly hung up the phone.

What kind of place was this, anyway, where the newspaper printed articles that were only half finished and then suspended publication so that its star reporter could spend the winter in Florida with her mother? For that matter, what kind of newspaper ran a headline like "Sea King Returns" and expected people to take it seriously? What kind of reporter was *she,* trying to track down the source of a ridiculous story like that, and getting mad enough to do serious damage to a public telephone booth when she couldn't?

She was restless, she was frustrated, she was homesick. She was tired of feeling helpless. She needed to be back where the action was, solving problems, getting answers, seeing results. Instead, she was stuck out here in some no-name backwater, mooning over a man with no background and no visible means of support and whose only verifiable character reference was over a hundred years old. No wonder she was going off the deep end over some crazy legend about a Sea King.

Well, there was one thing she could do. There were some answers she could get. Mr. Sean Seaward—if that was indeed his real name—could play his mysterious little games all he liked but one thing he would have to learn sooner or later was that no one kept secrets from Molly Blake.

With a grim set to her mouth, Molly dug through her purse for her address book, snatched up the receiver again and punched out another set of numbers.

A disgruntled male voice answered on the other end, reminding Molly that, in some circles—particularly those in which long hours were worked mostly after midnight—life didn't begin until after ten o'clock a.m. She used to belong to one of those circles herself.

"Red, it's Molly Blake. I know it's early but—"

"Office hours are from nine to five." The last words were muffled as though he was already moving the receiver away from his face.

"Don't you dare hang up on me!"

"Give me one good reason I shouldn't."

"Because I'm standing in a phone booth with a broken ankle in the middle of nowhere and I'm running out of quarters."

Only a slight hesitation. "And this affects me how?"

"Damn it, Red, I'm serious. I have a job for you."

He snorted with laughter. "Yeah, well, when you can get that fancy paper of yours to part with two hundred an hour plus expenses, you give me a call back. That Pulitzer Prize you're always promising to win is *not* going to pay my rent."

"Two hundred? Since when did you give yourself a raise?"

"Cost of living, babe. Somebody's got to foot the bill and it sure ain't gonna be you—that I learned a long time ago. Now, if you're finished ruining a perfectly good night's sleep—"

"Red," she said on a breath, "this is personal."

She knew he was not going to hang up now. She and Red went back a long way, and the favors they had done each other over the years were so numerous and so intertwined no one could keep track anymore, despite what Red would like to make her believe. In fact, they might even have become lovers if they hadn't been—as Red liked to point out—so damn much alike.

"Oh, yeah?" he said cautiously.

She could picture him sitting up now, reaching for a pen and pad.

"The name is Sean Seaward," she said. "Early- to mid-thirties...." She gave him a brief physical description, doing her best to leave out subjective adjectives. "He said his family is from this place called Harbor Island and has been for generations, only nobody around here has ever heard of him. He has a background in sailing or marine studies. He might have construction experience—check the unions."

"Got an address?"

"No."

"Car?"

"No."

"Employer?"

Molly swallowed before she spoke, knowing exactly how all this must sound to Red. It sounded the same way to her. "No."

He was silent for a moment. "And what is it you want me to find out about this guy?"

She drew a breath. "Everything."

"I see." His voice was even. "You've got no address, no social security number, DMV records or date of birth, am I right? You're not even sure this is his real name."

"Right."

"Then let me ask you this... Are you sure this guy even exists?"

Molly let her gaze wander aimlessly across the misty morning streets of the sleepy little village, and she sighed. "Not really."

She brought her attention back to the conversation at hand. "Look, I think he lives on his boat or sleeps on the beach, I don't know. Apparently, he had an ancestor by the same name who was a fairly well-known local artist. He might be an art collector himself."

"On which side of the law?"

"I don't know."

She could hear pen scratching on paper. "Anything else?"

"I don't know. Like I said, he seems to have a background in marine studies—check the universities, service records, the merchant marine."

A muffled groan. "Do you know what you're asking?"

"Yes. But you've done more impossible things."

"It's gonna take some time."

"I know."

"Look, I know you said it was personal, but I've got to ask."

"No you don't."

"Is this dude trying to run a scam on you?"

Anyone who knew Molly would have expected an indignant, heated denial coupled with lengthy assertions of how she was impossible to scam. So, no one was more surprised than she at the reply that came out of her mouth.

"I don't know."

Red's silence was stunned. Then he said, "Serious, huh?"

Molly answered again, in a slightly more subdued tone of voice, "I don't know."

"Do you need me to come down there?"

"No," she answered quickly. "No, and I don't want anyone to know I've brought you in, either. It's a small town and we need to keep a low profile on this."

"I'll do my best, sweetie. So where is this burg, anyway?"

They talked for a little while longer, arranging for him to contact her through the paper when he completed his investigation. Molly hung up, expecting to feel smug and satisfied for having taken the first positive step toward solving the mystery and regaining control of her life. Instead, she felt sneaky and miserable, as though she had betrayed the trust of a friend.

Chapter Eight

Sean wasn't there when she got home and Molly was glad. She kept telling herself she hadn't done anything wrong. He refused to tell her anything about himself so she had every right to use any other resources at her disposal to get answers to her questions.

It wasn't as though she had committed a crime, after all. It wasn't even as though she were doing anything new. She was Molly Blake, and she cracked cases, solved mysteries, got answers. That was just the way it was.

Thus reassured, she determinedly pushed away her residual guilt and settled down at her desk. For the first time since she had arrived on the island she pulled out her box of clippings and notes and settled down in earnest to do the work she had come to do.

The sea breeze whispered through the open windows, ruffling the papers and photographs spread out around her as the soft morning shadows gradually shortened and gave way to a room filled with cheerful afternoon light. Delilah settled down in her customary "working" position at Molly's feet and the keyboard keys clacked a bright determined rhythm. Words flowed like the tide to the shore; inspiration had never been smoother. It was almost as though the sea itself were speaking to her, providing the background for the words she wrote. Though she didn't really stop for introspection, Molly couldn't help observing that if she could have conditions like these in which to work all the time, her productivity would increase by one hundred percent.

She lost all track of time, and was startled by the voice at her shoulder.

"That's fascinating," Sean said.

Her heart sputtered and skipped a beat before resuming an almost normal rhythm. He was standing beside her, long tanned legs lightly dusted with dark hair below the hem of his white shorts, bare feet tucked into canvas shoes. Every sinew and muscle of his legs seemed familiar to her, as though longing had imprinted them on her brain: the swell of his calf, the sharp bones of his ankle, the shape of his knee.

She knew she had it bad when just looking at his legs could make her hungry with lust.

His head was bent at a thoughtful angle as he read over her shoulder from the monitor, his hair falling forward to shadow his face, long lashes lowered. He had a beautiful profile, the sharply defined jawline, sensuous lips and strong forehead would make any woman catch her breath on first glance. There was nothing wrong with Molly's hormones. Of course she was attracted to him.

The only question was, why was she fighting it so hard?

Molly cleared her throat, suddenly self-conscious. "I didn't hear you come in."

"The door was open. I called, but I guess you didn't hear." He looked over the photographs that were spread over the desk. "Are these all politicians?"

"Most of them. I was the Washington correspondent for the *Globe* before I settled down in Philadelphia to investigate crime and corruption. I got to know a lot of people. Some of them," she said, separating the photos, "are celebrities—singers and actors and serial killers with bestselling books."

He raised an eyebrow. "You've had an interesting life."

She shrugged. "It's not over yet."

His eyes, that breath-robbing shade of clearwater green, seemed to caress her through and through with a smile. "So it isn't. And who knows? Maybe the best part is yet to come."

For some reason, those words—or maybe it was just the way he looked at her—made her breath grow shallow in her chest. "Who knows?" she agreed, holding his gaze despite the pounding of her heart.

He sat on the edge of her desk, one foot resting on the floor, the opposite hip intriguingly close to Molly's hand, which still lay near the keyboard. He picked up a stack of photographs and began to sort through them. "How did it happen," he inquired, "that you chose Philadelphia in which to live the most recent part of your interesting life?"

It was hard to focus on his words, when his body was taking so much of her attention. "Chose? I didn't really. You go where the work is."

"This is your work," he said, indicating the computer screen. "It seems to me you've had no trouble bringing it with you."

"This?" She made a dismissive gesture with her hand, and her fingertips accidentally—or perhaps not so accidentally—brushed the material that covered his thigh. "This isn't work, just a hobby. Some memories and anecdotes I thought would make a quick book. No, I'm a newspaper reporter."

"Why can't you put this in the newspaper?"

"Do you mean like a column?"

The thought struck her with the innate charm of any new and perfectly simple idea. No more fighting traffic and smoky workplaces, no more two a.m. calls from a source and seven a.m. meetings at which the source failed to show. No more stories lost to a sagging budget or failing advertisers, no more bones broken in the line of duty. To just sit here and write about what she thought and what she knew while the sea breeze caressed her skin and the surf sighed in the background....

With an abrupt shake of her head, she drew herself out of her reverie. She *was* losing her edge. Not only her edge, but her mind, to even be considering such a thing. How did he do that to her, make her contemplate the impossible as though it were perfectly practical?

"I'm a reporter," she repeated firmly. "I need to be where the action is, getting answers, chasing leads, digging out the truth... making things happen."

She recognized in her words an eerie echo of the thoughts she had had earlier in the day as she'd tried to justify her investigation of Sean. She felt an uncomfortable rush of color touch her cheeks and she quickly avoided his eyes.

"Why?"

She looked back up at him, startled for a moment. "Why what?"

"Why do you have to be where the action is? What are you trying to prove?"

Molly's lips parted for one of her pithy, to-the-point replies and found she had nothing to say. She should have been insulted, indignant, and she was. Only, when he asked the question, when she looked into his eyes, it all seemed perfectly reasonable and she had no defense.

He was changing her, enchanting her, awakening things inside her she had never guessed existed before. Making her think about things that had never occurred to her, forget the things that were important. She looked at him and she had no answer.

She looked at him and all she could see was the color of his eyes, like lights playing on the bottom of a Caribbean sea, and all she could remember was the magic he had worked on her senses last night with a breath, a touch, a kiss. She looked at him and she could feel desire swelling, slow and thick, heating her skin.

Deliberately she moved her eyes away from him. "Stop doing that."

"What?"

"That thing with your eyes."

There was amusement in his tone. "What thing?"

"That mesmerizing thing."

He laughed softly. "Afraid I'll drag you off to my home beneath the sea?"

Molly scowled, running a hand through her tangled curls. She felt foolish. "To tell you the truth, I don't know what you might do."

He surprised her by bending down and taking her chin between his fingers, lifting her face to look at him. The amusement was gone, his expression was sober. "Nothing that you don't want me to. That is a promise."

A prickling sensation went through Molly's skin, though whether it was from the electricity of his touch or something else entirely she couldn't be sure.

"What do you want from me, Sean?" she asked hoarsely.

His index finger moved up, lightly tracing the shape of her lips. It was all Molly could do to keep from parting them, tasting his skin with her tongue.

"Not much," he answered softly. "Your heart, your body, your soul . . . your trust."

For a moment, he held her suspended, enraptured by his touch, his tender gaze, the sound of his voice. And then he smiled and moved his fingers away, and the moment was gone.

When he released her chin, Molly tore her eyes away from his, her heart beating too fast. She swallowed hard. She tried to restore normalcy to the moment. She couldn't ignore the fact that he was sitting just inches from the reach of her outstretched fingers, so close she could feel his heat, inhale his scent.

When she could trust her voice again, she spoke. "You weren't here when I got up this morning. Pressing business?"

He smiled at her obvious attempt to gain information about him. He stood casually. "The truth is, unless you're willing to undertake a major renovation, there's not much left for me to do here." A twinkle came into his eyes. "I'm running out of excuses to be near you. So tell me, Molly, what can I do for you?"

Once again her heartbeat sped up and a pleasant girlish excitement tickled the pit of her stomach. He was flirting with her and he was good at it. She didn't know him, she couldn't trust him, everything about him frustrated and alarmed her...but she couldn't stop herself from wanting him. She couldn't help flirting back.

"That's a leading question."

"Maybe I intended it to be."

And before she could react to that with more than a slight clenching of the muscles of her stomach, he suggested, "How about dinner?"

"Oh, I— That would be great, but I'm embarrassed to let you cook for me again. You've done so much."

He grinned. "Why do I think that's just a polite way of saying you don't care for my cooking?"

Molly relaxed, returning his grin. "I'm never polite."

"That I can believe. Anyway, I hadn't intended to cook. I thought you might like to get out, drive up the coast for seafood."

Dinner. A restaurant. A real date. But even as she registered the possibilities with a rush of surprised excitement, her reporter's mind latched on to something else. "Oh, do you have a car?"

"Sorry. You don't mind driving, do you?"

"Oh." She was sure he could hear the disappointment in her voice. Well, she was disappointed, but not because she minded driving but because a man with a car was a man who could be traced. She was right back where she'd started.

"No," she added, and smiled because she really *was* looking forward to dinner. "I don't mind at all. What time?"

"Early. I'll give you a couple of hours to finish up what you're doing and be back about five."

He started toward the door.

The words were out before she could stop them. "Where are you going?"

Faint amusement sparked in his eyes as he glanced at her over his shoulder. "To the beach. I'd ask you to come, but..." He gestured toward her cast.

Molly could have bitten her tongue. "Look, I didn't mean that to sound possessive—"

"Just curious."

"I'm usually not like that. I hate people like that."

"Incorrigible, you mean?"

She scowled, half in irritation with him, half in disgust with herself. "You don't exactly bring out the best in me, you know."

"I've noticed. I'll be back in a few hours."

He whistled for Delilah and, without a backward glance at her mistress, the wolfhound bounded off beside him as he left the house.

IT DIDN'T TAKE Molly a couple of hours to finish up her work. In fact, she gave up trying to concentrate less than fifteen minutes after he had gone. The rest of the time she spent getting ready for her "date."

She showered and shampooed her hair. She tried on all four skirts she'd brought, with an infinite variety of T-shirts and sweaters. She wished she had brought a dress. She wished she had brought a bra. No, she was better off without either.

More than once she stood in front of the pitted and wavy mirror in the bathroom and said out loud, "I can't believe I'm doing this. And for a guy I don't even know." A guy she had, in fact, turned over to a private investigator only that morning. *Any* guy, for that matter. What was the big deal with this date?

She was still contemplating that and other soul-wrenching questions—like whether to wear the blue earrings or the silver—when there was a knock on the door.

"Oh, no, he's early," Molly muttered, casting both pairs of earrings aside. Then, positioning her crutches for the limp to the door, she added, "I can't believe he knocked."

She opened the front door and a small blond female in bright pink slacks and turquoise-rimmed glasses swept in as though blown across the threshold by a gust of wind. Her hands were upraised, her face a transport of happiness; she looked as though she were in the throes of a religious experience.

"I can't believe it!" she cried. "It's here! *I*'m here! Oh, it's just like I imagined it."

Molly staggered away from the door, staring, as the little woman made a beeline for the fireplace. "Oh, just look! Doesn't it all send chills down your spine? How do you stand it?"

It took Molly a moment to realize the woman was primarily enchanted by the painting over the fireplace, although her superlatives did seem to more or less include the entire house. She stood looking up at the painting, her hands clasped together at her lips, her eyes shining, obviously enraptured—or insane.

"Who the hell *are* you?" Molly asked.

The woman turned, her face glowing, and rushed to Molly with hands extended. Molly took a cautious little hop backward on the crutches.

"I'm *so* sorry!" she exclaimed. "I'm Anna Christianson. Mr. Ritter at the general store said you were looking for me. And you're Molly Blake, I've read your stuff. Do you *know* how lucky you are to have this place?" She whirled, arms extended as though to embrace the room.

Molly took a quick hopping step forward. "You wrote that article in the paper—the one about the Sea King."

"And you're living in his house!"

Molly stared at her. "What?"

"My dear, don't you know?" Anna came forward, her expression excited and awed. "This is his house, his *place.* This is where he always returns, and this is where—" she lowered her voice confidentially "—according to legend, of course, he's going to finally find his true love."

"Wait a minute." Frowning with confusion, Molly balanced more securely on her crutches. "Are you telling me this Sea King is a real person?"

"He used to be," she replied confidently. "At least, so they say."

"Lady," declared Molly, "you are a nut." With a grand sweeping gesture of her crutch, she indicated the door. "Now, if you'll excuse me..."

"Oh, my dear!" Giggling, she covered her mouth with her hands. "I suppose I must sound terribly strange. It's just—being here, in this house, why the history of it! And that painting!" She whirled to face the fireplace again. "I mean, the rumor has always been that it was still here, but to actually see it—"

She broke off with a happy sigh.

Molly was cautiously interested. She put the crutch back on the floor, but remained ready to raise it again—in self-defense if necessary. "What do you know about the painting?"

"Well—" she turned back to Molly enthusiastically "—supposedly, it's a self-portrait, painted on his last return. You see, each time he returns he displays a new skill. Music, painting..."

"Carpentry," murmured Molly.

And at the other woman's bright, curious look, she flushed a little, feeling foolish. She was also hopelessly intrigued.

"Listen," she said, in a slightly more hospitable tone, "the reason I wanted to talk to you was to discuss the article you wrote, the one about the return of the Sea King. It was fascinating, but it seemed—unfinished."

Anna shrugged, turning back to the painting. "The paper only has so much room, you know. Some of it might have been cut."

"Some pretty important parts, I'd say."

She looked at Molly with a polite, curious expression. Molly tried a different tack.

"What about the name on the portrait? I thought this Sean Seaward was a real artist."

"Well, he was, wasn't he?" she explained reasonably. "For a time—until he failed to find his true love and was called back to the sea."

Molly impatiently tried to extract the kernel of truth from the nonsense. "You're telling me that Sean Seaward, the artist, never really existed?"

"The records are very scanty," she replied with deliberate vagueness. And then she smiled. "That's what makes the legend of the Sea King so enchanting, don't you know? It's so very easy to believe."

"If you're a nut," muttered Molly under her breath.

Anna cocked her head toward her. "I'm sorry?"

Molly tried again. "So Sean Seaward never had any descendants who remained on the island?"

"Goodness, I should say not! That *would* be odd, wouldn't it?"

"This is important. You're sure—"

Anna looked at her patiently. "My dear, I have lived here all my life, and all my folks before me. I've been writing for the paper for thirty-five years. I am *the* authority on who's who and what's what on Harbor Island, especially when it comes to history. I can assure you, nobody by that name has ever lived here."

Molly fell thoughtfully silent. In the distance, she thought she heard the faint echo of thunder, and the day seemed a little darker.

"So let me get this straight. You're telling me this whole legend of the Sea King got started when this Sean Seaward—"

"Oh, no, it began much earlier than that. Centuries, in fact." She gave a little gasp and reverently approached the ship's wheel that was propped up in the corner beside the fireplace. "Do you suppose— Oh, it can't be!"

"What?"

"But it must be! The wheel from his ship," she explained to Molly, touching the wheel softly. "This place should be a museum."

"What ship?" asked Molly impatiently.

Anna turned back to her. "The story is that the Sea King was once a sailor, a master of his craft, until he lost his life far too young during a terrible storm. Now, there are many theories about how this happened, and also about exactly what happened next, but the upshot of it is that the spirits of the sea, loving him as they did and regretting his early demise, granted him a second chance. Once a century, he could return to land and resume his human life—but only for a season. If at the end of that time he hadn't found his one true love he would be condemned to return to the depths of the sea, and there await the coming of the next century."

The similarities between this story and the one Sean had told her were undeniable, which of course raised a great many questions. Molly could focus on only one. "A season? How long is that?"

Anna smiled. "I can see you're not from a fishing community. Here on the island everything is governed by seasons—tourist season, fishing season, winter season."

"And you're telling me this used to be his house?"

"So the story goes."

A sudden gust of wind swept from the open back windows through the open front door, scattering Molly's papers and bouncing the door against the wall. They both looked outside toward the rapidly fading light.

"My word," observed Anna, "I do believe it's clouding up." She turned to Molly with a smile. "I don't want to leave you thinking we're all crazy. We're just terribly proud of our local legends, that's all—probably because we don't have much else to be proud of! And this house..." Once again she looked around with a gratified expression. "You're awfully lucky to have it. If these walls could speak... Well."

With a decisive squaring of her shoulders she turned toward the door. "I'd best be on my way before I get caught in a downpour. I knew this weather was too good to last. It's usually miserable this time of year."

"But your article," insisted Molly, "all that stuff about the fishing and the dolphins and the temperatures..."

"Well, of course. Everyone knows those are all signs of the Sea King's pleasure." At Molly's expression she chuckled. "I know it sounds strange to an outsider. But as I said, we live very close to nature here. And when for centuries you've depended on the whims of the sea for your survival—well, I suppose certain superstitions are inevitable. The kinds of things that have been happening these past few weeks really are phenomenal—we've had people from two or three oceanographic institutes up here studying them—but to the locals, it's all just a sign of the coming of the Sea King. Like the coming of Jack Frost."

Anna glanced worriedly out the windows again as another gust of harsh cold air rushed through the cottage. "Speaking of which, it looks like His Highness is blowing up a foul mood. I really have to get going." She extended her hand to Molly. "Thank you for letting me intrude like this. I hope I haven't left you with *too* bad an impression of us islanders."

Molly shook the other woman's hand absently, but wasn't quite ready to let her go. "Listen," she said. "I have to ask you something."

Anna waited expectantly and Molly took a deep breath.

"Is there any reason that a man who looks exactly like the one in the picture—"

Anna turned her head to look at the painting again.

"—should go around calling himself Sean Seaward and claiming he's always lived here and once was a sailor and talks about this house as though it was his own?" Molly finished in a rush.

Anna slowly returned her gaze to Molly. Molly knew exactly what the other woman was thinking. She'd thought the same thing about Anna when the woman had burst through the door.

"You've met such a man?" Anna asked cautiously.

Molly said nothing.

Anna gave her a long, skeptical look. "Because if you have," she said slowly, "times being what they are and people being what they are... What I mean to say is, with you living up here all alone... Well, there are an awful lot of strange folks around, aren't there?"

Molly felt angry heat stain her cheeks, anger at herself and the circumstances and the foolishness she felt. That she, Molly Blake, ace reporter, should have to receive a lecture on personal safety and gullibility from a ditsy grandmother in hot pink pants... that she *deserved* such a lecture, and that she had no defense against it—it was humiliating. Simply humiliating.

"On the other hand," Anna said, obviously searching for the bright side, "it could just be one of our local boys trying to play a trick on you. Of course—" she glanced again at the painting "—there aren't too many boys around who look like *him,* are there?" She gave an exaggerated sigh. "My, he's good-looking."

Thunder cracked and wind whistled, startling them both. Anxiously, Anna looked out the door and then quickly back to Molly, forcing a smile. "Well, it's been a pleasure. Perhaps I'll see you when I get back. Do take care now."

Molly murmured something polite in reply and fought to close the door behind her as Anna ran toward her car. By the time Molly got the door closed, raindrops the size of small pebbles were spattering the roof, and the wind that tumbled through the house felt like the beginnings of a small typhoon.

Gasping with exertion and struggling with the crutches, Molly turned to begin closing up the rest of the house. Sean was standing behind her half-way across the room, his face as dark as thunder, his eyes churning like a stormy sea.

"You couldn't leave well enough alone, could you?" he demanded.

Distant thunder rattled the rafters, echoing and echoing. Delilah whined and crawled under a table, upsetting a stack of magazines and several pieces of bric-a-brac in the process.

Molly stared at him. "How long have you been there?"

"Did you find your answers, Molly? Are you happy now?"

The anger in his eyes, the accusation in his tone, only fueled Molly's simmering outrage. She was the one who had almost believed him, after all. *She* was the one who'd made a fool of herself. She was the one who had fallen for him like a sacrificial virgin at the feet of a god.

"How dare you eavesdrop!" she snapped. "You should have—"

"How dare you go behind my back!"

"How else was I going to get any answers? You lied to me!"

Wind roared through the back windows in a furious rush. The remaining photographs and papers on the desk went soaring into the air as though slapped aside by an angry hand, and a volley of rain pounded the roof. The shadows inside the room abruptly deepened.

Sean's voice was like ice. "I never lied to you."

Though the gathering gloaming made it increasingly difficult to see, the tension that radiated from him was as electric as the storm that surrounded them. His eyes snapped like distant lightning, his face was as dark as a thunderous sea. If Molly hadn't been so outraged and insulted she might have actually been afraid.

"You've lied about everything," she cried, "from your name to your occupation to your family history! You've lied and I've *let* you lie! God, I can't even believe that you're standing here lying again and I'm listening to you!"

The thunder that cracked this time sounded like an explosion; it rattled glassware in the cabinet and caused lamps to shake on their pedestals. The rain that lashed against the windows, momentarily blurring everything behind a wall of water, was as thick as a crashing wave. It soaked the floor and everything in its path as the wind blew it into the house. For a wild moment, as she automatically shrank back and smothered a cry of alarm, Molly thought it might actually *be* the ocean, disturbed to such a fury that it would leap the cliff to get to Molly's house.

And despite all this, Sean didn't even look around. His hands were clenched at his sides, his voice low but clearly heard above the cacophony of the storm. "Who told you this, Molly? Who is it who says my name is not my name and my history is not my history? Whose truth do you choose to believe over mine? That silly woman's in the pink pants? Your friend down at the general store? Whose?"

"You don't get it at all, do you? *I*'m the victim here, not you! For God's sake, I *still* don't know who you are or what you're doing here! You could be a serial killer or a thief or a rapist—"

"Or even an eccentric millionaire with a yacht anchored offshore," he said coldly.

Molly gasped. "You—you *spied* on me!"

His laugh was bitter and mirthless. "An oddly ironic objection, coming from you."

Lightning flashed, catching in his eyes a cold light Molly had never seen there before, or imagined to see. Then she was afraid. Afraid she'd made a mistake, afraid she'd gone too far, afraid she was wrong . . . afraid of losing him.

Gripping her crutches tightly, she took a halting step forward. "Why?" she insisted, pleading with him. "Why did you have to be so mysterious? Why wouldn't you just answer my questions?"

It was completely dark outside now, a cold and empty darkness. The storm groaned and roared, battering the little house pitilessly. No lightning flashed for illumination, no thunder broke the empty echo of rain and wind. The bleakness outside was only a reflection of the desolation inside—in his voice, in his eyes, in Molly's heart.

"Because," he answered quietly, "I had to know if you were the one. I thought you were, but I guess I was wrong."

He turned then, and before Molly could call out or utter a word, he walked out into the storm.

Chapter Nine

The rain did not stop, and Sean did not return.

For three days, the winds and rains battered boats in their moorings, ripped down signs and traffic lights, tore off shingles and shutters. The sea rose to threaten beach houses and flood streets. The power went out and for three days Molly read by candlelight and burned driftwood in the fireplace.

The locals said the Sea King was displeased.

Molly spent hours standing by the window, looking for Sean.

It was ridiculous, really. She was grieving over a man she barely knew, with whom she had never even made love; a man who had lied to her, deceived her and then managed to make *her* feel guilty for being suspicious. A man whose voice, sweeter than the sweetest music, still haunted her dreams, whose touch could turn her skin to molten gold. A man who, in the short time she had known him, had made her question who she was and what she was and how she had always viewed life...and had almost made her wish she could be different, a better person than she was.

Everything he had done for her had been to help her; everything Molly had done had caused him trouble.

Eventually, the storm died down into a cold gray drizzle. The power came back on. Molly tried to work on her book but found her style had changed; she wrote a great many thoughtful, philosophical pieces about people and places and most of them featured the sea in some way. She wondered what Sean would think of them.

Over and over again, her attention was drawn to the painting over the fireplace. She couldn't count the number of hours she spent staring at it. In a strange way, it made the loneliness more bearable; in another, the painting was a poignant and painful reminder of what she had almost had—and lost.

Delilah was in a perpetual state of mourning. Every morning, the dog would walk to the end of the boardwalk in the rain and spend a long time just looking down at the ocean. Then she would turn and dejectedly trudge back to the house, where she spent the remainder of the day lying in the kitchen with her head between her paws.

Molly understood how she felt.

After a week, Molly donned her rain gear and drove carefully into town over rutted, water-damaged roads. The eyes of sullen, out-of-work fishermen seemed to glare at her from behind the lighted windows where they had gathered, sheltering from the rain. The Sea King had turned on them, and to Molly's overwrought imagination it almost seemed as if the townsfolk blamed her.

She had no friends here. This wasn't a pleasant place anymore. So why didn't she just leave?

"So why don't you just leave?" demanded Hal over the telephone line after ten minutes of listening to her complain.

"Because," she said, "I've got another three weeks of vacation left. I'm just hitting my stride on the book, and besides, I think the bridge is washed out."

And what if Sean came back? How would he find her?

That, of course, was the real reason and the only reason that mattered, and it embarrassed her. She added quickly, "Besides, the cast comes off next week and I'm not leaving here before I get a chance to walk on the beach, even if I do have to do it in the rain."

She muffled a sneeze as a draft of cold air crept in under the glass of the telephone booth.

"If you get pneumonia, don't expect any more time off," Hal said dryly. "So the book is going well, is it?"

Now she was a little uncomfortable. "I don't know. It's different from what I usually do. It might not be any good at all."

"Why don't you send me a couple of chapters and let me see what I think?"

She was surprised. Hal's moments of generosity were few and far between and should always be seized before he changed his mind. "Well . . . yeah, okay. Maybe I'll do that."

Wiping a trickle of water from the back of her neck—the roof of the booth had a leak—she added, "Look, what I called for was to check if I had any messages."

"What am I, your secretary? Don't you have voice mail?"

She had, in fact, erased some two dozen voice-mail messages before calling him. No one had anything to say that interested her in the least. "Presidents and potentates hardly ever leave messages on voice mail," she retorted. "They might just prefer to speak to my managing editor."

"Well, I can assure you that all presidents and potentates who called have already been assigned to other reporters. Who were you expecting to hear from, anyway?"

She sighed and hoped he didn't hear. "No one. But if someone did call—"

"I'd send you a telegram," he replied a little brusquely. Obviously, it had just gotten busy around there and his time for socializing was up. "Now, if you'll excuse me, I have a newspaper to run. Anything else?"

"No." Briefly and intensely, she missed the hustle and bustle of the office, the ringing phones, the clacking keys, the shouting and the rushing, the perpetual smell of newsprint. She missed it. Then why didn't she go home?

Hal added in a slightly gentler tone, "Call me in a couple of weeks, okay? And don't forget to send those pages."

"Right. Thanks, Hal."

Next she dialed Red's office. She hated herself for doing it but couldn't have stopped herself for the world.

"Anything?" she demanded.

"Come on, kid, you know how I feel about giving out incomplete information."

"Then you *do* have something."

"I didn't say that."

"Have you even started working on it?"

"Do you have another quarter?"

"What? No. Why?"

"I'm hanging up now," he replied in a singsong voice.

"No! Wait! Wait, Red, I'm sorry. I don't mean to tell you how to do your job. It's just that— Well, he's disappeared."

He was interested again. "Did you file a missing person's report?"

"On whom?" she insisted. "His name was one of the things I wanted to find out, remember?"

"Good point."

"Besides, as far as I can tell, the only person he's missing from is me. Possibly because I'm also the only person on this island who even knew he existed."

"Do you suspect foul play?"

The easy way in which he asked that reminded Molly all too poignantly of the life she had left behind. Where Red came from, foul play was the first thing that leapt to mind when a person disappeared. In this place, however, it was almost inconceivable.

She knew then why she wasn't in any hurry to go home.

"No, nothing like that," she said. "I'm just . . . curious, that's all."

He blew out an impatient breath. "Then why are you bothering me during working hours? I'll get it to you when I have it. The end. Goodbye."

He hung up the phone.

Everyone, it seemed, was living busy productive lives except her. And the most frustrating thing was that Molly could have been doing the same. Except she didn't want to.

She wanted to look into a pair of sea green eyes and feel herself tumbling into the light. She wanted to be touched by his smile and caressed by his voice. She wanted long quiet hours just knowing he was near. She wanted the sun to shine again.

But it didn't.

IT WAS a bleak foggy morning when she drove to a walk-in emergency clinic in Jefferson to have her cast removed. She had expected to feel lighter than air; she had envisioned celebrating this day with champagne while she ceremoniously burned her crutches in the fireplace.

But the doctor advised her to continue using the crutches for another week or two, while gradually accustoming her newly mended bones to her weight, so burning the crutches was out of the question. Besides, she didn't feel particularly celebratory.

She kept remembering the night she had first met Sean. The near tumble on the steps, being swept up into his arms and carried through the fog like the heroine of a Gothic novel. The days that followed, Sean offering his arm, picking up her crutches, helping her to stand....

If it hadn't been for the cast, she might never have gotten to know him, and certainly they would have never met. Who would have thought she'd actually have cause to be grateful for a broken ankle?

And now that she was healthy and whole again, she felt a little sad, as though a passage in her life were drawing to a close.

She mailed some of her favorite pieces from her book to Hal, and then immediately regretted it. None of them were very good. They were sentimental and self-indulgent and didn't really even belong in the book she was supposed to be writing. That book was a pithy and exacting study of life in the fast lane; what she had written were irrelevant little portraits woven around the people of this island, the stories she'd found in the books and magazines that cluttered the house, observations on nature and the rhythms of the sea. Hal would hate them. She was embarrassed.

Besides, she had lost interest in the book. All she seemed to want to do lately was sit and watch the dark and restless movements of the ocean.

When she returned to the cottage, she walked with Delilah to the end of the boardwalk in the drizzling mist and sat for a time in the shelter of the gazebo, watching the ocean churn and surge below. The sea was the color of her melancholy: black-green and frothy gray.

Delilah walked to the top step, looked back at Molly expectantly, and then started down. After a moment, Molly shrugged and said out loud, "Why not?" To judge by its performance lately, the weather might not get much better than this and this could be her best chance to walk on the beach. There was, after all, not much point in staying here any longer. She was getting no work done, and the constant drizzle was depressing her.

She followed Delilah down the steps carefully, using one crutch for balance on her weak side. After all, if she slipped this time, there would be no one to catch her.

Delilah bounded off across the beach, kicking up tufts of wet sand, pausing occasionally to look back at Molly as though inviting her to play. Remembering how Sean used to run with Delilah on the beach and toss sticks for her to play with, she smiled wistfully. Then she felt a prickle of angry resentment against him on Delilah's behalf, much like a mother whose child had been disappointed by an adult. After all, he'd made the dog look forward to their romps across the sand, gotten her accustomed to his special attention—then deserted her. It wasn't fair.

Molly left her crutch at the bottom of the steps, rolled up the cuffs of her jeans and started across the beach. Little needles of wet sand, thrown up by her sneakers, prickled her ankles. The wind was cold and steady, parting her hair and penetrating her sweater, driving a mixture of sea spray and rain into her face. The surf rumbled and crashed, spilling its dirty foam toward her thin-soled canvas shoes.

"Why did I ever think this was going to be fun?" she muttered.

But, ever determined, she picked up a piece of driftwood and whistled for Delilah. As the dog raced toward her Molly tossed the stick toward the tide line. Delilah raced after it, splashing into the surf despite the fact that the stick had come to rest half a dozen yards up the beach.

"Delilah!" Molly called, grimacing at the thought of drying off the huge, wet dog. "Come here!"

She threw another stick and Delilah followed it with an interested expression in her eyes, then turned and splashed farther into the water, nipping at the foam with her teeth.

"Great," she groaned. To the dog she called, "Get soaked then! See if you get any sympathy from me when you come whining to be let in the house!"

Delilah looked back at her and barked in cheerful defiance. The water was up to the top of her legs, which for a dog as tall as Delilah, was quite deep.

Molly took a concerned step forward. "Okay, girl, that's enough. Come on, let's go back!"

Delilah ignored her, ducking her muzzle playfully into the water.

"Delilah, come!" Molly slapped her thighs invitingly. "Let's go home!"

A swell lifted Delilah off her footing and caused her to dog-paddle for a few yards until she touched bottom again. Molly shuddered at the mere sight. "At least one of us can swim," she muttered. "Fortunately, it's the one in the water."

"Delilah!" she called again. And when the dog didn't even look around, she shouted, "Goodbye, Delilah! I'm going home!"

She turned with pretended indifference and started walking toward the stairs.

Her heart was stabbed by an ear-shattering canine scream.

Molly whirled just in time to see a tangle of paws and fur being tossed head over tail by a huge breaker. She screamed, "Delilah!" and stumbled toward the tide line.

A frantic yelp was her only reply, and in a moment Molly could see Delilah's head appear on the surface. She was beyond the breaker now but obviously out of her depth, paddling determinedly and going nowhere.

"That's it, girl," Molly cried. "Come on, come this way!"

Running but limping madly, Molly tried to stay parallel with the dog but the tide was fierce, it was an almost impossible task. Icy water swept over her ankles, soaking the cuffs of her jeans and slowing her down, filling her shoes with muddy sand. Her injured ankle began to stiffen up; she tripped in the sludgy, dragging water and went to her hands and knees, landing hard.

When she looked up again, Delilah was gone.

Molly's heart was in her throat; she couldn't even call out. Desperately, her eyes searched the water, like a jerky slow-motion camera shooting frame by frame, and each frame was punctuated by the slamming of her heart. Dark churning water. Huge angry breakers. The tide sucked and pulled and tossed and heaved but did not relinquish its prisoner.

"No," she whispered numbly. And then she screamed, "No!"

Splashing through the shallow tidal pool, wet jeans and sneakers dragging her back with every step, she stumbled into the surf. "Delilah, I'm coming! It's okay, hold on! Delilah!"

A wave broke against her knees, chilling her to the bone and sending a splash of choking saltwater into her face. For one horrifying moment Molly could feel herself being sucked in, the water swirling higher and higher, dragging her body down into its cold, black grave...covering her arms, her breasts, her neck, filling her mouth and her nose and finally her eyes, swallowing her as it had swallowed Delilah, paralyzing and devouring her.

Molly sobbed out loud and stumbled backward. She couldn't go any farther. She couldn't save Delilah. Held motionless by her own terror, she could only stand and watch helplessly as the angry sea rose and fell, dark and empty. Tears etched a hot path down her cold cheeks.

And then she saw something in the distance, floating on the surface. No, two things. Swimmers. Or one swimmer, carrying or towing something.

Her heart started to beat again. Not just to beat but to thunder. Her vision pulsated with the power of it even as she strained to see. Hope and dread filled her chest and she couldn't breathe. The swimmer drew closer.

Sean. And beside him, struggling bravely to keep her head above water while he guided her toward shore, was Delilah.

She thought she was hallucinating. She stared and stared and she thought her poor grief-numbed brain was only providing what she wanted to see and that made her even sadder.

And then a large breaker tossed the figures closer. Suddenly, Delilah fought her way clear of the wave, barking and scrambling for purchase on the wet sand as she ran toward Molly.

With a cry of inarticulate joy, Molly collapsed to the ground with a bundle of wet fur and enthusiastic kisses. She was sobbing, hugging the soaked and shivering dog and scolding her at the same time. "Oh, you bad dog for scaring me like that! Oh, good dog, good dog, yes, you're such a good dog! Don't ever do that again!"

Delilah wriggled out of her mistress's grasp and shook herself, spraying Molly with seawater and sand. Through the blur of saltwater and her own tears, Molly saw a pair of naked male legs, water slick and sand sprinkled, appear beside her.

And suddenly, with no further warning whatsoever, she burst into loud, helpless sobs.

Sean sank onto the beach beside her. From somewhere he produced a blanket, big and thick and woolly, and he drew it around both of them.

"It's all right, Molly." Music. His voice was music. "She's fine, just exhausted. She's safe now. You're safe."

"I thought— But the water, I couldn't go after her, I can't swim! I was so afraid, I couldn't— I couldn't move! God, I hate myself! I'm such a coward!"

"You're not. Hush, you're not."

His arms encircled her, he drew her close. He was naked beneath the blanket, his body salty and wet, but warm. She was shivering, her sodden clothes clinging to her like ice packs, chilling her to the bone. His heat, in comparison, was like the warmth of the sun and instinctively she drew closer to it, trying to draw it into herself, trying to pour herself inside him. At the same time, she pounded her fists against his naked chest furiously, crying, "Where have you been? Why did you leave like that? How could you—"

He caught her face between his hands and tilted her face to look at him. She was caught by his eyes, as deep as the bottom of the sea, as rich as jewels. Her breath died in her throat. Her skin tingled. The shivers dissolved into a slow warm glow. She melted into his kiss.

First his breath, then the warm sweet interior of his mouth. She tasted him, she was consumed by him. Sparks of light played upon her nerve endings, swept her into outer space, sent her spiraling into the deep dark well of passion. Breathing seemed a frivolous and irrelevant activity. She existed only for him and the sensations he made her feel, the magic he created from the inside out, the promise of more.

"Am I dreaming this?" she whispered. "I must be dreaming this...."

But his face, through her haze of passion, was clear and present. The dark hair with its distinctive white streaks was slicked down against his skull, curling at his collarbone. Droplets of water still clung to his skin. His eyes were alive with a dark hot fire in colors she had never known, mesmerizing colors, soul-stripping colors. He was the most real thing she had ever seen. And he was a vision.

He drew her against him again. "I tried to stay away." The words were murmured against her neck, the mere timbre of his voice sending spirals of desire through her that tightened the pit of her stomach. "I should have stayed away."

"No..."

"Molly, love. Just let me hold you...."

She sank into him, letting him cover her, absorb her, fill her with promise. Her head spun. *Molly, love*... He had called her *love*.

And then he moved away slightly, holding her face in his strong warm hands, his breath fanning her, his eyes searching hers. And he said huskily, "I won't do this. I won't take away your choice."

You already have, Molly thought dizzily.

And then he leaned forward and kissed her lightly on the lips. He smiled, though it was a forced smile that did not soften the heat of sheer desire in his eyes. "You're wet and cold. You should change your clothes and dry off. If I recall..." His muscles seemed to relax fractionally, and he lowered his hands. "I still owe you dinner."

Reluctantly, Molly let him draw her to her feet. "Come with me," she said hoarsely. "Come with me to the house."

He drew the blanket around himself. "As soon as I'm dressed."

Now, separate from him, Molly felt the bite of the wind. She shivered, but refused to move another step until she was sure. "Do you promise?"

And he replied soberly, "I never say anything I don't mean."

This time, Molly believed him. She had no choice.

She turned toward the steps, where Delilah was already waiting. And then, with a small gasp and a smile of delight, she turned back to him.

"Look!" she said, pointing.

The sun had broken through the clouds.

He smiled back.

Chapter Ten

Molly dried Delilah, gave her an extra large portion of dog chow and left her snoozing before the fire. By the time she emerged from a hot shower and dressed quickly in a sweater and long cotton skirt, he was waiting for her.

He had changed into dark jeans and a chambray shirt, and was wearing leather moccasins and no socks. His hair was soft and glossy, waving over his collar, his skin smooth and golden, eyes as rich as velvet. And still, looking at him, she felt a little disassociated, as though none of it were quite real.

As though she couldn't quite believe her good fortune.

"You look...great," she said, swallowing hard because she wanted to say so much more.

She wanted to ask where he had been, how he had happened to come back at such a propitious moment, why he was swimming nude in such arctic, stormy waters and where he had hidden his clothes.

She wanted to ask why the sun shone when he smiled.

He extended his hand, his eyes going over her appreciatively. "So do you."

Channel swimmers, Molly thought. *Sometimes they condition themselves by swimming in the nude in icy waters. So do other athletes. There are a bunch of crazy men in Michigan who go running through the snow and jump in the lake every winter. It's not so unusual. Obviously, he saw Delilah was in trouble and he swam to rescue her. He left his clothes on the beach along with the blanket.*

He was back, that was all that mattered.

She put her hand in his and said nothing.

They drove through a gold-sparked, lavender and blue late afternoon to a quaint clapboard inn about ten miles up the coast. Molly wasn't sure whether it was the fact that it had been so long since she'd seen the sun that made the quality of the light so spectacular, or her own inner joy, but she could not remember a more beautiful drive.

They were seated in a cozy dining room with dark paneled walls and plank floors, tables double-skirted in dark blue gingham with starched white toppers. They sat beside a big window where the setting sun turned the beach into a mirror of shattered gold that reflected off the indigo sea.

That was when Molly experienced her most severe case of disbelieving wonder yet. Only hours ago, the day had been as cold and bleak as the inside of her heart. A stormy sea had threatened and terrified her, and Delilah—the only truly steadfast friend she had ever had—was in mortal danger, thought lost.

Now, as if transported in time and place, she sat across from this man, this most incredible man, in a charming little restaurant that smelled of fresh bread and gourmet seafood, watching the sun set in a spray of colors over a quietly rolling sea.

It was magic, and Molly was heady with the awesomeness of it.

She looked at him, sitting across the table from her, so tall and graceful and stunningly good-looking, and she felt a swell of possessive pride that surprised her. She had read something once about the stages of courtship, in which "going public" was the most important. She thought she understood now why that was.

This was the first time Molly had ever seen Sean outside the very limited environs of the cottage or the beach. Being here with him now was more than a validation. It was an affirmation.

She said impulsively, "This means a lot to me, Sean. I don't think I realized how much until just now."

He looked puzzled, but pleased. "Dinner?"

"Taking me out to dinner," she qualified. "It's—well, it's hard to explain." And she gave a deprecating little turn of her wrist. "This is the first time we've ever been anywhere together. It makes you seem, I don't know, more real, somehow."

He smiled and lifted his water glass. "I'm not sure it's more reality you need, Molly. I was hoping to contribute to your fantasy life."

She felt a delicious heat suffuse her cheeks, a girlish grin forming on her lips. She lifted her own glass in a salute. "You do that, believe me."

Twilight progressed in shades of gray and lavender. The waiter lit the candles in their little brass stands. They ordered grouper and ate salads. She watched the way the candlelight brought out red highlights in his hair, and admired the strong bones in his wrist when he lifted his fork. Once again she experienced a wave of that this-is-too-good-to-be-true feeling.

"When did the cast come off?" he inquired.

She shrugged, a little self-conscious. "Today."

"The new look becomes you."

The way he smiled, even with so small a compliment, made her knees feel weak. She tried to concentrate on the salad.

"I celebrated a little early, I guess. That's what I was doing on the beach in that weather. I should have had better sense."

"Prudence was never your strong point."

She put down her fork and said sincerely, "I don't want to sound too sentimental, but I haven't thanked you for saving Delilah. I know she's only a dog, and not a very bright one at that, but she's the closest thing to a family I have. I'm glad you were there."

"Not nearly as glad as I am."

His voice. His eyes. How could anyone not fall in love with this man?

The thought startled her, and for a moment she did not recognize it for what it was, nor was she able to admit what it might mean. Perhaps to distract herself, or perhaps because she simply couldn't help it, she said abruptly, "Sean, I have to explain something to you."

He gave her an attentive look, and she folded her hands in her lap. She took a breath.

"I told you about my father. You didn't ask why he was in prison and I appreciate that. But I'd like to tell you, if you don't mind."

"Whenever you're ready."

Molly took a sip of her wine, trying to adopt a casual attitude. "It's not something I try to keep secret," she said with a small shrug. "Of course, I don't brag about it, either. The thing is, most people automatically assume that it's some kind of white-collar crime or even an injustice. I don't know. I guess they think people like me—people who hold down regular jobs and pay taxes and eat in the same restaurants and go to the same parties they do—don't have criminals for fathers. But I do."

She met Sean's eyes. "I grew up never staying in one place long enough to memorize my address. Trailers, basement apartments, once my mother and I lived six months in our car. My father was a bum. An alcoholic and a gambler, but mostly just a bum. He couldn't hold down a job, couldn't stay out of trouble. He thought the world owed him a living. He's been in and out of jail his whole life. This last time was for armed robbery. And the worst part is, I think, that my mother kept going back to him. Oh, there were a whole string of men in between—not one of them much better than he was—but every time he'd get out of jail, there she'd be, waiting to take him in."

She sipped her wine, trying to disguise her growing discomfort. "I guess you might say I learned to look for the worst in people at an early age. I know I got a good taste of the gritty side of life, which is probably why I ended up doing the kind of work I do...being comfortable with the kind of work I do."

"Exposing the seamy underside of life," he provided.

She met his eyes. "And enjoying it."

He nodded. "Because every time you expose a corrupt politician or a hidden criminal, you're striking a blow for that little girl who never had a father."

Molly frowned a little, genuinely uncomfortable now. She wasn't at all sure she liked how that sounded. She wasn't sure she liked how true it was.

"I guess what I'm trying to say," she said, "is that this is me, the way I am. It goes deeper than just my job. Suspicion is in my nature. I have to ask questions, I have to find out, I have to make *sure*. I didn't mean to invade your privacy, but when someone acts mysterious or evades my questions, it's like waving a red flag in front of a bull. I can't stop myself."

"I can understand that."

Molly took a deep breath. Having gone this far, there was no point in holding back. "But—it was more than just being curious. I was attracted to you. After a while, I was *very* attracted. And...well, you could have been a thief or a con artist or a beach bum.... God knows, you never did anything to make me think you were anything else."

She tried to smile, feebly. "I know it sounds small of me, but I wasn't sure I was prepared to form a relationship with an unemployed shell gatherer. Not at my age, anyway."

"Or a criminal," he added seriously.

Molly dropped her eyes. "Right."

The waiter removed their salad dishes and served the grouper. Neither spoke until he was gone. Even then, neither picked up a fork.

It was Sean who broke the silence. "My parents have been gone a long time. I don't remember much about them, except that my mother used to tell fairy tales in such a way that it was impossible not to believe." A brief reminiscent smile crossed his face. "That ability to believe in fairy tales is probably the most important gift she ever gave me. I want to share it with you, that's all."

Molly shook her head a little sadly. "It's too late for me to change. I can't stop being the way I am."

He reached across the table and covered her hand with his, giving it a gentle squeeze. "And neither can I."

Their eyes met and held for a long time. An understanding passed between them on the wings of a promise. And then, before the message in his eyes became too intense—or her own became too easy to read—Molly dropped her gaze.

Molly didn't really remember what she ate, only that it was the best food she had ever put in her mouth. And every time she looked up and saw Sean sitting across from her in the candlelight, her heart did a slow spin that left her as giddy as a child on a Ferris wheel.

They had coffee and a rich creamy dessert. Afterward, Sean asked, "What would you like to do tonight?"

Molly knew exactly what she wanted to do tonight and the thought made her head spin again. But she answered with only part of the truth.

"Walk on the beach," she said. "You know, that's all I've wanted to do since I came here, and now that I can, I mean to take advantage of it. I hope it won't be too cold."

"It won't be," he promised.

He took the check and they went to the cashier's desk to pay.

Molly had turned away, her attention caught by a book on coastal inns, when she heard the cashier say, "Excuse me, what is this?"

"It's payment for dinner," Sean replied. "Have I given you too much?"

The young girl was staring helplessly at the coin in her hand. An older man came up behind her, took the coin and examined it, blank faced.

"I'm sorry, sir." Politely, he returned the coin to Sean. It looked to be made of gold. "We can't accept this."

"Do you have any idea what that is?" Sean said just as politely.

"Some," the man replied. "And if I'm even close in my guess, we don't have enough cash or goods in this building to make change." He looked narrowly at Sean. "Do *you* know what it is? And I wonder if you'd mind telling me how you came to have it?"

Molly moved forward quickly. "Um, here, I have a credit card."

As far as Molly was concerned, the clerk couldn't imprint the card fast enough. She scrawled her name on the receipt and grabbed Sean's hand, hurrying outside.

"I apologize," he said. "That wasn't very chivalrous of me. Please, keep this as a gift."

In the light of the street lamp, Molly stared at the coin in her hand. It had an unfamiliar queen on it, and the writing looked like Spanish. It appeared to be in mint condition, and it was heavy, solid gold.

Her throat was dry. She said hoarsely, "Do you know how much this is worth?"

"Quite a bit, I should imagine. Enough to make that clerk in there spend the rest of his life regretting what he just did."

"I did a story on sunken galleons once." She raised her eyes to him slowly. "Some of the coins they recovered were worth twenty thousand a piece. Are you—are you a salvage operator?"

Sean reached into his pockets and brought out both hands filled with coins. Some were still encrusted with dried barnacles, black and tarnished. Others gleamed dully. There were all sizes, both silver and gold. There must have been two dozen. Molly could do nothing but stare.

"I have a chestful. More than enough to last a lifetime, several lifetimes," he said quietly. "I understand your insecurities, Molly. I am not a beach bum." And he smiled. "Nor am I a thief, as our friend inside seemed to think."

Molly raised her eyes from the coins in his hands to his face. "You're not going to tell me, are you?"

He smiled, returning the coins to his pockets. "You have the rules you must live by, so do I."

She looked down at the gold piece in her hand, turning it over, feeling its weight. She offered it back to him. "I can't keep this. It's too valuable."

He closed her fingers around the coin. "Please," he said. "Keep it. It's only valuable if, when you look at it, it makes you think of me."

Molly knew at least that much was true. Every time she looked at that coin she would think of him. Her only difficulty would be in controlling *what* she thought.

She released a long breath, shaking her head slowly in a mixture of wonder and resigned amusement. "You can't be for real," she said.

He leaned forward and kissed her lightly on the lips. "I can be," he assured her, "if you believe I am." And his eyes were serious as he looked at her. "I need you to believe in me, Molly."

She swallowed a sudden thickness in her throat. "I'm trying."

He slipped his arm around her waist as they walked toward the car. "That's all I ask."

THEY WALKED on the beach. Moonlight spilled like silver over Prussian blue satin waves, the breeze tugged at Molly's skirt and tousled her hair and stung her cheeks. There was a quality to the night that was fresh washed and clean, sparkling with energy yet hazy-soft and gentle. It was a night where anything might happen, imbued with magic because Sean walked at her side.

Their fingers were lightly entwined. They had left their shoes at the bottom of the steps and the sand was cool beneath Molly's feet. She knew she should be freezing but she wasn't even chilled. Could the temperature have risen that much or was it all in her imagination? Or was it simply Sean, and the heat he generated inside her simply by being near?

"It's funny, isn't it?" she said after a time. "That someone as afraid of water as I am should be so drawn to the beach."

"Not really." Moonlight played in his eyes, caught in his smile. "Perhaps you always knew I was waiting here for you."

Perhaps I did . . .

And then she forced herself back to reality. This was the moment she had dreaded, and she tensed inside as though to ward it off, but she knew she couldn't avoid it any longer. She had asked for total honesty from him; how could she offer him anything less?

"Sean, I need to tell you something else."

"All right."

His voice was smooth and musical, his fingers strong and comforting around hers. She wanted to cling to him, even as she knew what she had to say would push him away.

"I—have a friend who is a private investigator." She tried to get it all out in one breath. "I asked him to look into your background."

For one awful moment, he said nothing. The ocean continued to sigh and rush, the breeze continued to blow and they continued to walk along the shore. But the silence was the loneliest sensation Molly had ever known.

Then he said, in a tone that was part amusement and part surprise, "I know that. Is that all?"

She stopped walking, and turned to stare at him.

"It's a small town," he explained, totally unperturbed. "And have you gotten your report yet?"

"I— No. Do you mean you're not angry?"

"I *was* angry," he corrected, "and for that I apologize. I realize now I have no right to ask you to be what you're not, just as you have no right to ask the same of me. I am curious, though. What will you do with your report when you get it?"

She felt numb, stunned, and only part of the sensation had to do with the fact that his hands had settled around her waist, inching her close, thigh against thigh. The question was far beyond her ability to reason at that moment. "What?"

His eyes. She could drown in his eyes.

"Do you really want to know, Molly? When you open that folder and discover I'm nothing more exotic than an insurance salesman or an overgrown lifeguard, will you be pleased? Or disappointed? Will a social security number or a driver's license make me a better person? Or will it simply make me ordinary? And is that really what you want?"

She frowned a little, confused. "I— It's not a matter of being a better person. I never said that. And there's nothing wrong with being ordinary."

He smiled and kissed her lips lightly. "Isn't there?"

The only thing Molly knew was that he would never be ordinary. He couldn't even pretend to be ordinary when even so light a touch of his lips across hers could make the stars dance in the sky and fill her veins with molten honey.

She laid her hands atop his arms. She felt the shape of muscle and bone beneath the fabric of his shirt, the warmth of his skin. "I'm glad you came back, Sean."

He slipped his hands around her neck, fingertips dancing down her spine. His eyes were dark now, the color of the sea behind them, reflecting all its many subtle lights and shades. "So am I."

His face was close. She could feel his heat and taste his breath. Her hands slid upward, over his biceps, and her palms vibrated with an electric pleasure just from touching him. She parted her lips, not knowing what she was going to say. And even she was amazed by what came out. "I want to make love with you, Sean."

And he answered simply, "Yes."

"I have almost from the beginning."

"You never said so." His eyes were burning through her, igniting her skin.

"You knew it." She could barely whisper.

"I needed you to ask."

He took her hand and started to lead her toward the steps. She held back.

"No. Here. With the ocean and the wind and the smell of the sea . . . where you are. Where you belong."

"You'll be cold."

"Where is your blanket?"

He swept her off her feet and into his arms and the sky turned around. The sand and the surf and the star-studded night swirled together into one grand collage as he kissed her.

When she opened her eyes again, she was on the ground, the wool blanket cushioning the sand, a diamond and velvet ceiling high overhead. The ocean played a symphony of sound in the background. Sean knelt astride her, his knees cradling her legs, his hands entwined with hers. His hair fell forward, shadowing his face, and the only light she saw was in his eyes.

"Molly. So long. It's been so long. . . ."

He lowered his head and his mouth closed upon her throat, heat and moisture, deep and drawing passion. She arched helplessly into the sensation, threading her hands through the silky curtain of his hair. She drank in his scent, his heat, the essence of him that thickened the air like a smoky drug. She grew drunk on him.

Magic.

Over and over, that word came back to her. The magic of the elements and the pounding sea, of time distorted and whirling space, of sensations that were magnified almost beyond bearing, and then, incredibly, attenuated even more. The magic was in his fingertips, his breath, his eyes, his whispering voice. It was in his satiny skin and flexed muscles, in the dark moist recesses of his mouth and the secret hollow behind his ear and the salty taste of him, the scent of brine and wind.

She didn't know when or how their clothes were removed. She knew only the frisson of skin against skin, the infusion of heat, the pounding of hearts. She shaped his muscles with her hands, traced the veins and sinew, planes and curves, with her tongue. Visions danced inside her head, sea colors deep with passion—greens, silvers, blues, fractured light and swirling patterns.

His skin seemed to blend into hers, a slow electric molecular disruption that left her dizzy and filled with him, empty and aching for him. She felt his hair spilling through her fingers, his heartbeat pulsing against her breast, his fullness between her legs, pressing into her. She opened to accept him, drawing him in, absorbing him, becoming him.

Magic.

She kept thinking the word. Magic. She felt borne upon the wind and tossed by the tide. She was outside herself and more of herself than she had ever been before. She was part of him and he was magic.

The physical sensation racked her body and spun her to dizzying, breath-robbing heights. Yet sensation seemed so small a part of the experience that physical fulfillment peaked and passed and still she clung to him. She turned him on the blanket, feeling him grow strong inside her again until the rhythms of love and sea overtook them and they made love again, and again.

She couldn't let him go. She couldn't return from where he had taken her. She couldn't let this end.

And when at last her body failed her and exhaustion claimed her, she remained cradled in his arms, holding him tightly, waiting for the wonder to pass. It didn't. She was different. The world was different. She had taken him inside her, she had given up a part of herself to him and now they were blended, and it was impossible to separate one from the other. How could she *not* be changed after that?

Sounds were clearer, the air was purer, colors sharper. She could hear his heartbeat. She could hear the ocean rumble and roar, and the sound made her want to sing. She could see distant lights from some faraway boat on the horizon. She could see the tenderness in Sean's eyes. A sensation swelled inside her that was strange and beautiful and terrifying and huge. It was an ache, a joy, a need. The power of it made her shudder.

Sean drew her closer, shielding her with his arms and legs. "Are you cold? Shall we go in?"

She should have been cold. But the breeze felt tropical, balmy. "Not cold," she whispered. "Just... afraid."

The concern in his eyes was quick. "Afraid of what?"

Molly buried her face in his shoulder and tried not to cry. "Oh, God, Sean, I think I'm in love with you!"

She felt his long slow breath, the slow tightening of his arms. His lips touched her hair. His voice was deep and thick with emotion. "Thank you, Molly. If you only knew how I needed to hear that. I have adored you forever."

Forever...

Yes, that was how it felt. As though she had loved him forever... or as though loving him was the only reason she had ever lived.

She found his hand, threaded her fingers through it and fought fiercely to keep reality at bay. She wanted to believe in him. She wanted the magic to last. But she knew it wouldn't. How could it?

"Why can't it be easy?" she said softly. "I want it to be easy...."

After a moment, he disengaged his fingers from hers and took her face in his hand, tilting it to look at him. His eyes, so loving, so deep, so full of strength. Nothing could harm her when he looked at her like that. Nothing could take the magic from her.

"Then let me make it easy," he said gently. "My name is Sean Seaward, and what I told you about my ancestry is true. I'm an oceanographer from Boston University, and my crew and I are in a vessel anchored off the coast about a mile. There are several of us up here from different universities around the country, studying the unusual tide and migratory patterns that have been noticed in this area lately. It's that simple."

Of course. It was *perfectly* simple. Perfectly reasonable, perfectly believable, perfectly sensible. She should have thought of it before. Of course.

She waited for the sense of relief, the lifting of anxiety, the certainty to take hold. But it didn't, because as rational and reasonable as it all sounded, it wasn't... right.

She searched his eyes and found nothing there to confirm or deny her suspicions. "Is that the truth?"

He combed his fingers through her hair, his eyes moving over her face like a caress. He smiled. "Do you want to know the truth? Think about that before you answer."

But Molly didn't have to think, not really. She settled into the curve of his shoulder and closed her eyes. "No. Not now. Not this minute. Now... I want to hear a fairy tale."

"All right."

He kissed her cheek and lay back, his face turned toward the sky. His voice was like music. Molly closed her eyes.

"Once upon a time, there was an arrogant young man, born to privilege and aristocracy, accustomed to mastery in all things. He was cruelly beautiful and vain about his looks, but careless of women, using them and discarding them at will. He took to the sea at a young age, imperiously determined to master it as he had everything else. But the sea is a woman, too, and no more forgiving of a man's contempt than any mortal maid.

"And yet, I think, the sea was half in love with him, for she favored him with many a full sail and following sea before he challenged her once too often and earned her fury. He was swept overboard in a black squall, his life snuffed out as he was sucked into the bosom of the mistress he had scorned.

"But after a time, the sea came to regret taking the life of one so young—a life that had been so piteously wasted in vain pursuits—and remembering how she once had loved him, she offered him a second chance. It was a curse, and a promise.

"He was transformed into a creature of the sea, where his life would be spent in the normal way of such creatures. But once a century, for the space of a single season, he might leave the sea, and once again take on human form. This cycle must continue until he learned to love a woman, and found a woman who would return his love to the exclusion of all else. He could not cajole or charm or persuade her in any way. She must choose him of her own accord, and come to him freely. Only when he had found a woman who, through the greatness of her love, was willing to sacrifice everything for him and follow him into the sea could he be free of the curse."

He fell silent, and the silence lengthened. Molly's throat felt tight. She turned her face to look at him. "What happened?"

His smile was a little slow in coming. His eyes seemed sad. "That's the charm of this particular fairy tale. You make up your own ending. What do you think happened?"

Molly swallowed hard. "The sea...a mortal woman...she could drown."

"She would have to trust her lover not to let that happen, wouldn't she?"

"But she would have to sacrifice everything, even being human, for this man, for a world she doesn't know and can't imagine. That doesn't seem fair."

"Love is often unfair."

She looked at him helplessly, her forehead puckering. "It doesn't have to be. It shouldn't be."

He passed a soothing hand over her forehead, as though to stroke away the frown lines. "So," he said. "What is your ending?"

Molly shifted in his arms, snuggling close, but unable to meet his eyes. "I don't know," she mumbled. "Don't ask me that. I'm no good at this. None of my stories ever have happy endings."

He kissed the top of her curls gently. "This one could," he said. "It might be the only time in your life, but this one could."

Molly closed her eyes again and held him tightly and tried with all her might to believe it would.

Chapter Eleven

Molly had always taken life in greedy impatient gulps. But over the next few days she learned the exquisite pleasure of anticipation. Making love with Sean was more than just an hour's frantic passion. It began each day with the dawn's first caress and didn't end until she drifted to sleep at night to the sound of the surf whispering his name. She dreamed of magnificent sea creatures and white-columned palaces under the deep, for it was easy to believe no mere mortal could wring such delights from the body of a woman, could open her spirit to so many new wonders.

With Sean it was easy to believe in magic, and Molly knew that no matter what happened, she would be able to look back on this time for the rest of her life and know that once she had had that.

But Molly didn't think about what might happen. She didn't think about the future at all. For the first time in her life, she knew what it meant to be completely focused on the moment, to learn the lessons of nature and the rhythms of the sea. The stillness that lay on the world the moment before sunrise, the way the day spread like molten lava across an indigo sea; the call of a gull, the chitter of sand birds, the smell of salt on a clear autumn day.... Those were the things of which her life was made, and those were the things Sean made possible for her. When he went for his morning swim she accompanied him to the beach and watched as his long strong limbs cut through the water, her heart catching as he swam out of sight and then swelling with pleasure when he reappeared.

Because he knew she was watching and didn't like to worry her, Molly suspected he swam closer to shore and took fewer chances than he otherwise would have done, but ever so often exuberance would overcome him and he would dive like a porpoise through the waves or swim with a sudden breathless burst of speed until he was out of sight—only to suddenly break the surface in a place he could not possibly have been, laughing and waving to her and inviting her to join him.

There were times when Molly was almost jealous of his love for the sea, which seemed the one thing she could never share. And the sea, as everyone knew, was an equally jealous lover. Molly wondered how long it would be so generous as to share Sean with her.

Perhaps that was why, on this particular morning, when he waved to her from waist-high, silver-blue water, she was more tempted than ever to join him.

"The water's great!" he called, teasing her. "Come on in!"

His hair was as slick as a seal's, his face sprinkled with water droplets, his eyes as bright as foil wrapping paper. Naked and beautiful, he was a creature of the sea, and he called to her. Molly's heart sped with nothing more than the thought of going to him.

She was standing just out of reach of the tide line. Kicking off her sandals and draping her skirt over her arm, she ventured a few yards forward. The foam that licked at her toes was warm and playful, and she looked up at Sean, grinning.

Approval mingled with the pleasure that danced in his eyes. "Ready for that first swimming lesson?"

"Well now, I don't know about that." She was coy as she stood there, wiggling her toes in the damp sand. "Can you give it to me here?"

"Afraid not." The sea lapped at his chest as he extended his hand to her. "Come a little closer, Molly."

She looked at him, and her heartbeat felt heavy in her chest. Before her, the waves broke with noisy, foamy crashes. Any one of them could easily sweep her off her feet. And beyond them the water deepened and surged, reaching Sean's chest, occasionally causing him to rise to its rhythms. But because he asked her, she moved a little closer to the breakers.

"I'll get wet," she said, nervously winding the folds of her skirt around her hand.

"Yes," he agreed, "you will."

His hand remained steady, reaching for her. Molly forced herself to go another step, then stiffened as a small breaker crashed against her shins. The receding sand crawled beneath her feet, threatening her balance, and she stood absolutely still, now forcing herself not to run for the safety of shore.

"It's not deep, Molly. You can walk the whole way. Just tie your skirt around your waist." Then he grinned, trying to coax a smile from her. "Unless you'd like to run into town for a designer swimsuit, and then try it."

"That might be best," she answered shakily.

"Molly." There was gentle command in his voice, quiet strength in his eyes. "Come on, give it a try. I'm not going to let anything happen to you. Don't you trust me?"

She did trust him. She wanted to trust him. His hand was so far away. She ached to take it. She wanted to splash through the breakers, wade knee-deep, thigh deep, waist deep and be caught up in his arms... but she couldn't.

Another wave was arcing toward her, its eye dark and its curl frothed with foam. If it struck her it would knock her off her feet. She turned and ran out of the water.

After a time, as she stood on the beach ashamed and miserable, she felt Sean come up behind her. He took her shoulders and drew her back against him, massaging gently.

"I'm sorry," she mumbled. "You must think I'm an idiot."

"That's the last thing I think you are." He kissed her neck. "And hey, you're improving. The last time you wouldn't even get wet."

Molly relaxed, grinning. "You know something?" She turned, looping her arms around his neck. "I like you. A lot."

"The feeling is mutual."

His hands cupped her face, fingertips tracing her eyebrows, the shape of her nose, the corners of her lips. Gentle wonder filled his eyes as he did so, and he said softly, "Molly, this time I've spent with you, every moment of it—I just want you to know it's the happiest time I've ever known."

Molly sank against him with a sigh, molding herself into his wet skin, letting his emotion mingle with her own until she was filled to bursting with joy, with need, with wonder. "The feeling is mutual," she whispered.

And yet there was a part of her that knew deep down inside it couldn't last. Nothing that was good in her life ever did.

SHE WOKE UP one morning and opened the front door to inhale the new day. There was a yellow cablegram tacked to the doorframe. It read:

You're late.

Hal

Sean came up behind her, encircling her waist, brushing his face against her hair. Molly loved the feel of his hands, separated from her naked skin only by the thin material of her sleep shirt, and of his warmth cradling her backside. He smelled sleepy soft and tousled. She adored him.

She frowned at the telegram. "What day do you suppose it is?"

"I don't know. Sometime in November. The moon is in the third quarter."

She twisted around to stare at him. "November! How can that be?"

This was a bit more serious than oversleeping or forgetting a meeting. She was supposed to have been back in Philadelphia a week ago. Hal must be going crazy. How could she have lost *weeks* of time?

But she looked into Sean's eyes and she knew exactly how.

"Oh, wow," she said, turning back to the telegram. "I guess I have to go into town and call the office."

He kissed her neck. "I guess so."

He dropped his hands and stepped away. Molly felt suddenly cold, standing there in the doorway in her nightshirt. She shivered and went inside, rubbing one ankle against the opposite calf.

Philadelphia. Cold and gray and noisy. The smells, the sounds, the *business*.... It seemed like another world, one from which she wanted to recoil in distaste. Yet it was her world, the one to which she belonged...wasn't it?

She looked helplessly at Sean, who was kneeling by the back door, roughhousing with Delilah. He was wearing jeans and nothing else, laughing as he ruffled the dog's fur, and Molly's chest contracted painfully. They had never talked about this. Why had they never talked about this?

He knew she didn't live here. He knew she had a job to go back to. And he... Who could guess where he lived or what *he* had to go back to? They knew this time would come, of course they must have known it. Why had they never talked about it?

They had spent the past weeks in a fantasy world, timeless and insulated, where nothing existed except the two of them and the love they made together. There was no room for jobs or schedules or decisions that must be made. Sean had done that for her, that was his gift to her. He had shown her how to forget all that; he had built for her a world in which none of it mattered.

Suddenly, Molly knew she was not ready to leave that world.

"I'm going to call Hal," she said. "I'm going to ask for a leave of absence."

He opened the door for Delilah and sent her racing happily outside, barking for him to join her. He looked at Molly and smiled. "Whatever you need to do."

The response might have sounded cavalier to someone less observant than Molly. But she recognized the expression in his eyes, an agony of yearning and forced dispassion. It was the same one that had been there when he had said to her once before, "I won't take your choice from you."

Molly walked over to him and wrapped her arms around his neck, kissing him tenderly. "I need to do this."

She could feel the tension in his arms and back and neck. That he could not disguise from her, although he tried to do so with his smile and casual tone. "I think I'll run with Delilah on the beach, then go for a swim. I'll be here when you get back."

She tried not to be disappointed. She had wanted him to go with her. This would be the first time they had been separated since he had returned and she was foolishly superstitious about being away from him, even for so short a time.

He started to follow Delilah's imperious bark, until Molly called out his name.

He looked back.

She swallowed hard. "When I get back...we have to talk."

His smile had faded; his voice was quiet. "I know."

MOLLY DIALED her voice mail first and discovered, to her chagrin, that the tape was full. How many messages had she missed? She *never* did things like that. Could she possibly get any more irresponsible?

One after another the messages played, most of them not worth writing down, particularly considering the fact that she had no plans to come back to work any time soon. But one voice, a husky Southern drawl, surprised her.

"Molly, where the hell are you? Jeez, I hate a gal who won't answer her own phone. This is Renny. Give me a call." She gave a number with a Washington area code.

Renny was short for Renata Jenkins, Molly's college roommate and probably the best—if not only—female friend Molly had. The last she had heard, Renny was working at the White House. She copied down the number.

A few messages later, Renny's voice was heard again, more irritated now. "Good God, girl, are you dead? This happens to be important."

And even later: "If you're not tied up interviewing some head of state—or tied to a chair by one of your many enemies—I can promise you, you'll regret this for the rest of your life. You do not snub old friends in powerful places. Call me, damn it."

And Molly almost dropped everything and did so that very minute. But she had to deal with Hal first.

He picked up on the second ring.

"Hal, this is Molly."

He replied dryly, "Molly who?"

"Listen, I'm really sorry. Some things came up and— Well, what do you want from me, anyway? I haven't had a vacation in six years."

"Have you talked to Renata Jenkins?"

Molly was momentarily taken aback. If Renny had called Hal, it must be important. "No. Listen, she's not sick or hurt or anything, is she? I must have had half a dozen messages—"

"Just call her," he said flatly. "When you're done, we'll talk. Meanwhile..." His tone changed slightly. "About this material you sent me."

At first Molly didn't know what he was talking about, so far removed did that time seem from this. When she did remember, it was with a tingle of embarrassment. "Oh, that. It needs a lot of work. I was going through a kind of blue period. Experimenting, you know."

"It's different," he agreed. Then he shocked her by adding, "I like it. More importantly, readers like this kind of thing. What are you going to do about first serial rights?"

Once again, the statement was almost too much for her to comprehend. "What? I mean, why?"

"Because I'd like to buy them, Einstein. Have your agent call me. You are going to finish this damn book, aren't you?"

"I— Yes, well, sure. One day. I guess."

"Hmmph." His voice was gruff. "Well, if not, maybe you'd be interested in turning some of this stuff into a column. In your spare time, of course."

"In my— A column?" She tried to focus on the conversation, but it was extraordinarily hard to do. "What are you talking about? I'm a news reporter, aren't I? Am I fired? Are you that mad at me? Listen, I told you—"

He sighed loudly. "Call your friend."

And he hung up.

An odd sort of panic set in as she stared at the humming receiver in her hand. She had finally blown it. She had pushed him too far. A whole career, down the drain because she had *forgotten* to return from vacation. How could she have been so stupid? How could she have let this happen? She had spent years struggling to prove herself, clawing and scraping to get to this point and now it was all for nothing, wasted.

She forgot, momentarily, that the reason she had called Hal in the first place was to request an extended leave of absence.

She knew she was overreacting. Hal hadn't said she was fired. If she were fired, he would have said so. And what was all that nonsense about serializing her book, about her writing a column? And what in the world did Renny have to do with any of it?

There was only one way to answer the last question. She dialed the Washington number and was put through to her old friend after only a short wait.

"Well, can I believe my ears?" demanded Renny when she picked up the phone. "I was just making up a list of who to invite to your wake. Where've you been, girl?"

Molly sighed. "Long story. I just got your messages."

"Better late than never, I guess."

"What's going on?"

"Only the biggest break of your life. Only an offer that will have you kissing my feet for the rest of your natural life. Come home, sweetheart. Your future awaits."

Molly frowned, rubbing the back of her neck, which had begun to ache dully. "What are you talking about?"

"There's an opening on the White House press staff. The job is yours if you want it."

Molly felt all the breath leave her lungs, as though she had been kicked in the stomach. She couldn't say a word. She couldn't even think.

After a moment, Renny prompted. "That's *the* White House, sweetie. Washington, D.C.?"

Molly knew what it meant. Her old stomping grounds, the ins, the outs, the heady pace she loved. It was a dream come true. With a job like that on her résumé, she could virtually write her own ticket. The future was hers.

No wonder Hal had acted so strange. Renny had obviously talked to him. He knew Molly couldn't afford to turn down an opportunity like that. He knew he had lost her.

Finally, she croaked, "But I'm a news reporter. Why me?"

"Apparently, you didn't make as many enemies here as you usually do everywhere else," replied Renny breezily. "You're all set. The only problem is, we need you next week."

Now Molly gasped out loud, her thoughts racing. "Next week!"

"Well, you would have had more notice," replied Renny dryly, "if you'd only returned your phone calls."

"But I'm not even at home. There's so much to do. I can't possibly—"

"You *can* possibly," said Renny firmly. "I'll arrange for an apartment, you give your notice. Somehow, I don't think your boss will be very surprised. Oh, did I mention the salary?"

She named a figure that made Molly's knees go weak.

"So call me tomorrow with the details," Renny ordered. "Gotta rush. And congratulations!"

Molly supposed she murmured her thanks, or goodbye, or something. She didn't know how long she stood there holding the receiver and staring at nothing at all before reality finally returned.

She left the phone booth slowly and started for home. And Sean.

IT WAS AMAZING how one short hour could change everything. Even the world around her looked different; the beach didn't sparkle as brightly, the sky was not so brilliant nor the surf so clean as it had been before she left for town. She spent a long time standing at the top of the steps, looking down at Sean, who sat alone on the sand gazing out at the sea. It was as though he already knew what she was going to say when she returned.

Even Molly did not know that.

And suddenly she was angry. What had she expected, anyway? That the fairy tale could last forever? She knew things like that didn't happen to her; she had always known. And Sean had hardly made it any easier for her. What had he promised her, or even offered her? They had never talked about commitment or permanency or even tomorrow. They had created a world that couldn't possibly last. He knew that and she knew that.

Then why was it so hard to leave?

Delilah, sniffing along the beach below, saw Molly first and barked. Sean turned around. Molly lifted her hand to him and started down the steps.

He didn't stand up when she approached. He was wearing jeans and a cotton sweater, and sat with one arm resting across his upraised knees, tossing bits of broken shell toward the tide line. The wind ruffled his hair and moved changing shadows across his profile.

"It's getting late." That was all he said.

Molly didn't understand what he meant, and her silence told him so.

"Colder," he said. "Winter's almost here."

"Oh." Molly cleared her throat. "Yes."

He looked up at her. Certain knowledge was in his clear green eyes. "So," he said.

"So," she answered.

He waited.

And it all came out in a rush. "It's not what you think. I have a job offer—in Washington, back where I belong, in the White House, for heaven's sake. I have to at least talk to them about it."

He expressed no surprise, no disappointment, no anger. In fact, there was only the mildest interest in his voice as he inquired, "Do you?"

"Do I what?"

"Belong there."

She frowned. She could feel tension tightening her spine like a steel rod. Why didn't he say something important? Why didn't he beg her to stay?

"In Washington? Of course I do. I know people there, I did my best work there, I can get things done there. Of course I do!"

He picked up another shell, and tossed it toward the tide. "I want you to try to remember why you came here," he said carefully.

"I was hurt!" She heard the defensiveness in her voice but didn't know where it had come from. "I had a broken bone, I came here to heal!"

"Even though you would have been more comfortable in your own apartment with no stairs, and people to run errands and make deliveries for you."

"I was tired. I was working too hard. I needed to get away."

"You have been here for almost two months, with no telephone, no newspaper, radio or television set—no news from the outside world at all. The average person would have been insane by now. You haven't even asked who won the World Series."

Her fists tightened at her sides. "If you're thinking I'm burned out, that I can't cut it anymore—"

He shook his head, the ghost of a smile shading his lips. "I'm not saying that. It's that we all go through changes in our lives, when the definition we've given ourselves doesn't quite fit anymore, when maybe we're *not* what we always thought we were. Sometimes it's not easy to know when to let go and move on."

"I *am* moving on!" she insisted. "To Washington."

Until she said the words, she had no idea the decision was made. She hadn't intended to make it, not without talking to Sean, not without some serious soul-searching, not without carefully weighing the pros and cons. Not without giving Sean a chance to beg her to stay. But the look in his eyes told her he had known all along.

"Are you saying this is the wrong thing to do?" she said, desperately trying to backtrack. "That I shouldn't take the job, that I should get out of the business, that—"

"I can't make those decisions for you, Molly," he said gently. "I can't tell you who you are."

"No, of course not." She tightened her lips against the bitterness that was welling up in her throat. "You're not a part of my life. You never intended to be."

He didn't meet her eyes. "I wanted to be," he said in a low voice.

"Then come with me!" She dropped to her knees beside him, catching his arms, beseeching him. "I don't mean forever, just for a little while, just to see how you like it, just to give us a chance. For God's sake, Sean, I've spent two months in your world, can't you spend just a few weeks in mine?"

He looked at her sadly, and the silence seemed to stretch into forever. Then, finally, he said, "No."

Molly fell back. The pain couldn't have been more shocking and intense if he had slapped her.

His eyes softened. He lifted a hand as though to caress her, but she shrank back. "Molly, what good would it do? I'd help you move, get settled in Washington, you'd be making a place for me in your life even though I didn't fit there, and you'd hate me when I had to leave. I can't live in Washington. Stay here."

She'd ached to hear those words, begged to hear them, but now that he'd said them, they only made her angry. "How can you ask that of me?" she demanded. "That isn't fair! You want me to give up everything while you give up nothing! Why should I do that?"

He dropped his eyes. "No reason. No reason in the world."

"You haven't even given me a choice!" she cried, feeling angrier and smaller and more helpless by the moment. "You're a fisherman, a scientist, a beach bum— I don't even know *who* you are or where you're from or what you do, for God's sake! You avoid my questions and you tell me fairy tales. Then you ask me to stay with you, to give up my life, my career, my friends, my home—for *what?* A woman needs to know those things, Sean! This is not a game. My life is not a game!"

He said sharply, "I've told you—"

"Fairy tales!" she cried as she leapt to her feet. She stood looking down at him, breathing hard. "I can't live on fairy tales, Sean. No one could!"

The sun had gone behind a cloud, and the wind was cold. Delilah had abandoned her canine games and stood down the beach a little way, watching them worriedly. Molly shivered. She felt the bleakness right down to her soul.

She should have known. From the beginning, she *had* known it would end like this. How could it have ended any other way? She was who she was and he was who he was and there had never been a chance for a happy ending. She had always known that.

She stuffed her hands into the pockets of her jeans. "So. This is it."

He said nothing. He wouldn't even look at her.

Molly turned away. She couldn't say goodbye. She couldn't say anything at all, because her throat was already burning and aching and full to bursting—and no matter what, she wouldn't cry. She wasn't the kind of woman who cried at goodbye scenes. She had been through enough of them to know.

It was just that this time, she had been so close. She had wanted it so badly.

"Molly."

She turned, hoping, aching, hardly daring to hope.

"It was good, though, wasn't it?"

She tried to smile but all she could manage was a nod. "Yeah. It was." *The best. Only the best time of my whole life....*

But that was all it was. And now it was over.

She was almost to the steps before she heard his voice again. She thought her heart would break, right then, into two brittle pieces. She turned.

This time, he was on his feet, looking after her, his body held rigid as though fighting the urge to follow her. "If you change your mind, you know where to find me."

And that was the worst of it. "No," she said. "I don't."

She climbed the stairs, a cold wind stinging the tears that bathed her cheeks.

That was when she discovered she was that kind of woman, after all.

Chapter Twelve

Molly couldn't believe how white her new apartment was. White—and featureless and cavernous and empty. Even when all her furniture finally arrived, even with its spectacular view of the Potomac, it was empty. And white.

Delilah didn't much care for it, either. She had a four-floor elevator ride just to go outside. There was no beach to run on, no gulls to chase and no one to throw sticks for her. She spent most of her time lying on the white rug before the white marble fireplace or gazing out the big picture window at the river. The view seemed to disappoint her. Molly had to admit, it was no Atlantic Ocean.

"Well, I don't understand what the problem is," Renny said in that flat, direct way of hers. "You got a great job, great place, and you live in the most exciting city in the world. Don't you like the job?"

Molly shrugged. "It's okay."

She was unpacking dishes. Since she hardly ever used them, they were always the last things to be unpacked wherever she lived. Renny had taken advantage of the newly discovered cups and saucers and had made herself a cup of tea, which she now enjoyed from the comfort of Molly's sofa.

The truth was, Molly wasn't crazy about the job. Of course it had only been two weeks and she knew it would take at least a month to settle in, but she didn't think she would ever like it. Everything was so frenetic here, so urgent, so must-be-done-yesterday-if-not-sooner. She felt awkward, out of step, straining to catch up—and she didn't even much care whether she caught up. Had she ever found this sort of thing fulfilling?

She thought all this but verbalized none of it. "Actually," she said, "your boss is kind of a jerk."

"My boss," said Renny, peering at her over the rim of her cup, "is the president of the United States."

"Not him. The other one. Jacobson. Mr. Let-Me-See-What-You've-Got-So-Far."

Renny shrugged. "So he's a little retentive."

"Try a little nuts."

"That, too. But don't worry, you won't have to put up with him for long."

Molly unwrapped a cream pitcher. She couldn't imagine where she had gotten it, or what she thought she would ever do with it. "How come? Is he being transferred?"

"Heart Attack City," replied Renny confidently. "He's got it written all over him. His type come and go like trains. I give him six months at the outside."

Molly stared at her. "He's not even thirty-five years old!"

Renny snapped her fingers a couple of times. "They drop like flies around here. It's the pressure, you know."

"Great," Molly muttered. "One of the unexpected perks of my new job—decreased life expectancy."

"The way you've been acting lately, I can't really believe you'd even notice."

"What's that supposed to mean?"

"I mean you've been acting like a zombie since you got here," Renny said flatly. "I've known you ten years and I don't *know* you. What the hell is going on?"

Molly challenged sharply, "Is there something wrong with the way I do my job? Do you want to fire me?"

"It's less than inspired, if you want to know the truth," Renny retorted. "But I'm not going to fire you, mostly because that's what you *want* me to do. For God's sake, Molly, why did you take the job if you didn't want it?"

"I did want it," she insisted. And then, as the hollowness of the words echoed around her, she let her shoulders sag with defeat. She sank onto a chair, a piece of crumpled newsprint in her hand. "At least I thought I did."

She sighed. "God, Renny, I don't know. Nothing is like I remembered it. I thought it would be the best thing I'd ever done—to be in the center of the action, my finger on the pulse of the nation, to know every word I wrote would be read by people who mattered....

"But where the president is going tomorrow or what the secretary of defense said yesterday—it's really only as meaningful as this, isn't it?" She looked down at the wadded newspaper in her hand. "What people use to line their bird cages or wrap their dishes."

"So name me one thing is life that's *more* meaningful," demanded Renny.

Molly shrugged. "I don't know. It's all point of view, I guess. Whatever it is, it's got to be what *you* think is important. As for this—" she made a sweeping gesture toward the window, which was meant to include the city at large "—it just seems as though I've done it all before."

Renny stared at her. "You're a reporter. What are you supposed to do?"

And when Molly had no answer, Renny gave a shake of her head. "Girl, you're the *last* person I ever expected to go weird on me."

And then her eyes narrowed with quick perception. "Wait a minute. There's some man at the bottom of this, isn't there?" Her eyes widened with enlightenment. "Of course! She's moping around, can't concentrate, talking out of her head . . . she's in love! For heaven's sake, why didn't you just say so? You had me worried to death."

Molly felt instantly uncomfortable. "Don't be ridiculous. I don't fall in love. Not the way you mean, anyway. I'm too selfish to let a man rule my life that way."

Renny smiled and sipped her tea. "So who is he? Somebody you met on vacation?"

Molly shrugged, running a hand through her hair. She could feel that old familiar ache knot up under her breastbone with no more than the suggestion of the thought of him. It was an emptiness that was so intense yet so habitual it hardly even hurt anymore. Missing him. Needing him. Looking up and expecting to find him there.

She couldn't lie to Renny, as much as she would have liked to; in all their years of friendship, she hadn't even been able to keep a secret from her very well. "It was just one of those island romance things. You know, like the guy you meet on a cruise ship and you don't even know his last name?"

Renny gave an exaggerated lift of her eyebrows. "Maybe *you* pick up guys on cruise ships..." Then, "What's his name?"

Suddenly, Molly didn't want to talk about him. To say his name, to bring him into this place and time, made him real, made him possible, made him seem not quite so lost forever. She thought it would be better if he remained a fantasy, an ideal that was unobtainable and therefore painless.

"You don't know him." That was all she said. One line that would put an end to their conversation.

"Does that mean he doesn't have a name?" Obviously, Renny didn't catch her intent. Or didn't want to.

"Sean, okay?" she replied irritably, standing up again to resume her unpacking. "Sean Seaward."

"Hmm." Renny sipped her tea again. "I had a girlfriend who spelled her name like that, only she pronounced it 'Sayard.' They do, where she was from up north."

Molly turned slowly and stared at her. Seaward. Sayard. No one on the island had ever heard of him, or his family. Was that because she had been pronouncing his name wrong?

But Sean himself had told her his name. Surely *he* knew how it was pronounced.

Perhaps. But there was no reason that he should choose to give his name the regional pronunciation, particularly if he had not grown up in that area. Leon at the marina had known who he was. Sean had sold him a net. He had understood her when she said "Seaward" because Sean would have pronounced his name that way, too.

If all her doubts about him could hinge on something so simple . . .

But no. What was she thinking? That was crazy. Sean would have told her if that were the case. Molly's problems with Sean went much deeper than the simple mispronunciation of a name.

And what they hinged on was whether she chose to believe what he told her.

Molly turned away, confused, and dug in the dish barrel for more to unpack. "So what does he do?" Renny asked.

He makes the sun shine when he smiles. The thought came unbidden, and it embarrassed Molly.

"He's an oceanographer from Boston University," she blurted out.

Renny sounded mildly surprised. "Do they have an oceanography program there? I didn't know that."

Once again, Molly stared at her. One phone call, that's all it would take. The old Molly would have known that, would have seized upon it immediately. *You know where to find me.* One phone call.

Molly shook her head fiercely, as though by doing so she could also shake the thoughts of him out of her mind.

"He was insane," she said tensely. "He was always telling me these wild stories and doing these insane things. He swam naked in the Atlantic in the middle of a storm, for God's sake!"

Renny laughed out loud. "Sounds like just your type! A match made in heaven."

Molly scowled at her. "He would never talk about himself, he was always messing with my head. He'd make me so mad, I'd want to strangle him sometimes."

"Uh-oh. A man who knows how to handle you. This sounds serious."

"It wasn't serious," Molly said quickly. Too quickly. But her heart was beating hard. Just talking about him, bringing him from that world into this one, had stirred up longings in her that were almost more than she could bear. "He never talked about the future—God, he never talked about the past! He never promised me anything...."

Except love....

Her throat thickened and she had to swallow before she could go on. "He was completely unpredictable, totally incomprehensible.... It was as though he spent his days plotting ways to get under my skin."

"What's this?" Renny's voice was filled with mock astonishment. "A man you couldn't bully, control or manipulate? And you let him get away?"

Molly's scowl only deepened. "A woman would have to be crazy to let a man like that get to her."

"Isn't that what love is all about?" Renny got up and put a sympathetic arm around Molly's shoulders. "Being just crazy enough to let go and let it happen? I mean, you close your eyes, you hold your breath and you jump in when you can't even see bottom. Total surrender. If that's not crazy, what is?''

With a little squeeze of Molly's shoulders, Renny stepped away. ''We need to talk about this some more, sweetie, but I'm due back in the office in twenty minutes.''

Molly dragged herself back from the depths of swirling sea green memories long enough to register surprise. ''But it's Saturday!''

Renny shrugged. ''That's life in the big city. You're only getting weekends off because you're new in town.''

On her way to the door she stopped and glanced around the apartment thoughtfully. ''You need to buy some paintings,'' she said. ''This place is too white.''

Molly's eyes went to the blank space over the fireplace, where she could almost see a stormy dark sea and a man rising up from it astride a dolphin. She heard Renny say something else, but she didn't understand the words.

She dragged her attention back to her friend, who was poised beside the door. ''What?''

''I said, here's your mail.''

She held out a large manila envelope, which was how all her mail from her former office was forwarded. Molly came to take it from her. ''Thanks. I guess I didn't hear the mailman drop it in.''

"Mail*person,*" corrected Renny with a groan. "When are you hicks going to learn to be politically correct?"

She grinned, promised to call Molly later and left.

"Politically correct, socially correct, heart attacks before you're thirty-five..." Molly sighed out loud and sank to the floor in front of the fireplace, running her fingers through Delilah's fur. "Some great new life I picked for us, huh, girl?"

Delilah looked up at her, thumped her tail once and closed her eyes again.

Molly looked at the envelope in her hand but was almost too dispirited to open it. The Philadelphia address reminded her of Hal, and Hal reminded her of the cottage on the coast.

"That," Molly said out loud, staring at the envelope, "was the happiest I've ever been." She hadn't recognized it at first because it didn't seem possible that she, Molly Blake, could be happy living at the edge of the world with no television, radio or telephone and with the only newspaper one that headlined stories about mythical sea creatures.

But even now, if she closed her eyes, she could hear the sound of the surf, feel the wind moving like fingers through her hair, smell that clean salty smell that clung to his skin....

She opened her eyes abruptly because the pain was starting again, that awful empty ache. There was no point in looking back. She had made her choice. Hadn't she?

She focused on the envelope until the blurring in her eyes cleared and the stinging in the back of her throat went away. She ripped it open and spilled out the contents on the carpet.

Maybe...

The idea came from nowhere, startling her with its suddenness. Maybe Hal would sell her the painting of the Sea King. Why wouldn't he? He probably didn't even know it was there. He would sell her the painting and she would have a part of Sean, a part of that season they had shared, with her forever. Her memory could be real.

Excitedly, she reached for the phone, dragging it from the desk onto the floor with a little *clang* of the ringer. And then she stopped, staring at one of the envelopes on the floor. Everything seemed to stop.

It was a smaller manila envelope than the one in which her mail had been forwarded, but someone had folded it in half, anyway, which was why Molly hadn't noticed it before. The return address was Caffey Investigations.

Red. This was the report she had ordered on Sean.

She picked the envelope up cautiously, as though it might hurt her if mishandled, which, she supposed, was exactly the truth. It wasn't very heavy, three or four pages at the most. One page would be

Red's cover letter. That meant that what he had found was routine and unexciting—or that what he had found was nothing.

A man with a prison record would have a thick file. A university professor would have a thin one. A man who had never existed at all...

Do you really want to know, Molly? The voice was Sean's. *Will a driver's license or a social security number make me a better person...?*

Her hands were shaking. One small movement was all it would take, and the truth would come spilling out in her lap. One phone call to Boston University. One minute spent scanning a thin report and it would all be over. All her questions would be answered, all her doubts put to rest, and her life would be changed.

Total surrender.

Molly looked at the envelope for a long time. Then she leaned forward, opened the fire screen and dropped the envelope between two burning logs. She sat back and watched it go up in flames.

Her life was already changed. *She* had changed. That was what, until this moment, she had refused to recognize.

She picked up the phone and dialed the Philadelphia number, in the hopes that Hal would be there on a Saturday morning. Delilah, as though sensing something exciting was in the works, perked up her ears and watched.

"Hiya, Mol!" Hal greeted her when he came to the phone. "What're you doing bothering an old man on a Saturday morning?"

"What are you doing at the office on a Saturday morning?"

"No place better to be, I guess."

Well, I have some place better to be, some small hardly audible voice said in the back of her mind. *Now and for the rest of my life....*

"Say," Hall was saying, "Did you see it? The clipping I sent of your piece we ran last week."

Molly pushed aside envelopes and papers until she found it. It was part of the collection she had written at the shore; on impulse, she had agreed to let Hal pick out his favorites and run them as a limited-run column. *Seasons* by Molly Blake. They had even used a good photograph of her. She liked it.

"First response has been pretty good. Not to say that my instincts aren't always right on the mark, but it surprised even me. People are saying we need more thought-pieces like this, that the paper's got too much bad news. Well, I always say—"

"'I don't make it, I just print it,'" Molly chimed in with him, and they both chuckled.

"Miss you, kid," he said. "You wouldn't be calling to say you want to come back to work, would you?"

"No," Molly said. "But if you're serious about doing a whole column of my stuff—"

"If you've got more like what I've seen," he said quickly, "I'll run it for as long as you send it. You want a contract?"

"Later," she said. Her heart was beating slow and hard. She thought it was just from pleasure at his response. "What I really want to know now is if you would sell me your—"

Painting. That was the word she intended to say. She even heard it in her mind: *Painting*.

What she said was, "House."

"What?"

And then she knew that was exactly what she wanted, precisely what she'd meant to say, the only thing that made any sense at all. "Your beach house, on Harbor Island. Will you sell it to me?"

"Well—hell, Molly, this is right out of left field! What do you expect me to say? I mean, I know you're making a lot more now than you were at the paper, but you've only been there a couple of weeks. How can you afford this kind of expense?"

Molly slipped her fingers into her pocket and felt the reassuring presence of the gold piece. He had said it was only valuable if it made her think of him. But Molly knew what it was worth, and she knew it could bring her back to him.

"I've had a windfall," she told Hal. "Will you sell?"

Molly thought his hesitation was only for effect. "Well, I'll have to talk to Betty—"

But she could practically see the cash wheel turning in his head. A chance to unload that place at a profit—it was a dream come true for him. He wasn't about to say no.

"You do that," she said quickly. Her heart was beating harder now, faster. It was from joy, from celebration, from the relief of having done something right, the *only* right thing she had ever done in her life...but also from urgency. "And when you decide on a price, you have the papers drawn up and sent to my banker here. I'll give you the name and address. What I need from you now is the key."

"Key?"

"To the cottage. I want to go up there this weekend, today."

"Today?" he echoed, clearly stunned by Molly's whirlwind behavior.

Molly didn't blame him. She was a little stunned herself.

"I'll be in Philadelphia this afternoon," she said. "If you're not in the office, leave the key for me."

"I'll be here," he assured her.

Molly grabbed her coat, her purse and her car keys, whistled for Delilah and didn't look back.

Chapter Thirteen

It was spitting snow in Philadelphia when she arrived late in the afternoon. Hal tried to persuade her to stay overnight and complete the journey in the morning, reporting that the weather was only worsening up the coast. Molly couldn't wait, and she knew it sounded crazy when she couldn't give him a reason why.

She shivered and pulled up the hood of her coat as she stepped back out into the nasty gray day. *It's late,* she thought, running toward her car. *Winter's almost here.*

Those words, echoing in her head, caused her heart to stammer a beat before leaping into action again. She knew then the source of the urgency she felt. How long was a season? Would he still be waiting for her when she got there?

"All right, girl," she told Delilah, gripping the wheel hard as she swung out into traffic. "We're on our way. And this time, we're not stopping for anything."

But the car wouldn't go fast enough, the narrow coastal highways weren't quick enough to get her back where she belonged. The snow turned to sleet, then to driving rain, then to snow again. Up and down the radio band she heard weather reports:

"A driver's advisory has been issued for the area between Chickapee and Union City...."

"Hazardous driving conditions prevail as the coastal area remains under a winter storm watch...."

"Unusually severe weather conditions continue to dominate as storms hover over the Atlantic...."

I'm coming, thought Molly desperately. *Sean, I'm coming....*

When she left the main highway for the winding coastal road, the night was as black as pitch, unrelieved by street lamps or structures for miles, hours, at a time. Wind dragged against the car, slowing it down, battering from the side and occasionally sending it skidding on the icy pavement, flinging sheets of snow and ice against the windshield. There were times when the windshield wipers, working at full speed, could barely keep the windshield clear of snow, and a sensible person would have looked for a place to stop for the night, or at least pulled off the road to await the passing of the worst of the storm.

Molly was no longer sensible. She didn't think about blizzards or wind gusts or icy roads or stranded travelers. She kept driving. The snow turned to rain, blinding sheets of it in places, steady drizzle in others. The fog was so thick, she had to slow to a crawl. Delilah whined anxiously in the passenger seat. Molly's knuckles turned white on the wheel.

When she reached the Harbor Island Bridge, it was pouring rain again, a thick battering rain that sounded as though it was mixed with ice. A yellow highway department truck was pulled up in front of the bridge, its emergency lights flashing. Two men were just dragging the yellow-and-black Bridge Closed barricade across the road.

Molly stopped the car and got out. The wind flung needles of ice into her face and neck and ungloved hands as she pulled up her hood and ran in the beams of her headlights across the road to the two men.

"What are you doing?" she shouted. "What's wrong?"

"Bridge is flooded!" they called back. "You'll have to turn back!"

"But it's not!" Frantically, Molly pointed to the bridge where muddy water lapped at its edges, but did not quite cross. "It's not flooded!"

"The river's up! It could cover the bridge any minute!"

"I can get across, I know I can! I've got to! Please, move the barrier aside."

"Ma'am, we can't—"

"Please!" she cried. "You don't understand, it's a matter of life and death!"

My life, she thought desperately. *The rest of my life....*

The men looked at each other for a moment, then one of them said to her, "Hurry."

They moved the barricade, and Molly drove across with the river splashing beneath her wheels.

When she reached the cottage, it was dark and empty, as she knew it would be. She almost drove past it, in fact. If her headlights hadn't caught the broken sign—Gull Cottage—swinging in the breeze, she would have missed it entirely.

I'll have to tell Sean about that, she thought. *He needs to fix it.*

An ordinary thought, on an ordinary day. Add it to the list of Sean's things to do around the house. But this was no ordinary day.... And Sean—as he always said—was no ordinary man.

She parked the car and tumbled out, Delilah fast on her heels as she ran through the wind and needle points of rain up the walk. Somehow, with freezing, trembling hands, she got the key in the lock, fumbled open the door and burst inside.

"Sean!"

Her voice echoed.

She tried a light switch, then remembered the electricity had been turned off when she left. It was cold, icy cold, and as silent as a tomb. Delilah's nails clicked on the bare floor as she moved around, snuffling for a familiar scent. Molly could have saved her the trouble. He wasn't here. What had ever made her think he might be? Was she insane, driving all this way in the middle of the night on such a ridiculous notion?

But no. She wouldn't listen to that hateful little voice of logic. She had come too far and hoped too hard, believed too desperately. He was here. He was everywhere, in the rain and the wind and the sound of the surf. He was here and he would come back to her because she needed him, because she loved him....

She ran through the darkened house, checking every room, calling his name. Then, leaving Delilah inside, she went out into the cold and the rain, racing down the boardwalk. She checked the gazebo, where he had first kissed her. It was empty.

She turned and called into the wind. "Sean!"

The wind tossed her voice back to her.

She started down the steps.

"Sean!"

The night was black and the steps were steep. Rain stung her face and the icy wind tore tears from her eyes. More than once she almost missed her footing and tumbled to the rocks below.

And Sean was not there to catch her.

She reached the beach. The ocean was like thunder, roaring and crashing in her ears.

"Sean!" she screamed. "Where are you?"

She turned and cried again. "Damn it, you said I'd know where to find you! I'm here, Sean! Where are you?"

Nothing answered except the pounding of the ocean.

She turned to the tide and shouted again. "Sean! Don't leave me here alone! I won't let you leave me here alone!"

She pulled off her jacket and dropped it onto the wet sand. She kicked off her shoes, one by one, stumbling toward the tide line.

"Sean!"

By the time she reached the water, the wind and rain had chilled her through, and she didn't think it was possible to get any colder. But when the icy surf washed over her bare feet and soaked the cuffs of her jeans, the impact sent a shock through her that caused her to cry out loud with pain. She fought the urge to retreat to the cottage, and went on. She struggled for footing as another wave crashed against her calves, sending icy spray up to her thighs. She fell to her hands and knees, gasping for breath while brittle shards of ice stabbed through to her bones.

She was soaked to the waist and sobbing with cold. She pushed to her feet and stumbled forward, into the angry gray-black surf. "Sean!" But her voice was hoarse and barely audible above the sound of the crashing waves. "Sean, I'm here!"

She was shivering so ferociously, she could hardly form the words. "I've come to you—of my own free will! I want to stay with you! Sean!"

She couldn't feel her legs anymore, though she kept dragging them forward, pushing them forward against the tide. The joints in her hands and arms screamed with protest when she moved them, the pain went through her like a knife. The water was over her waist now, hurting her chest where her heart pumped desperately to keep her warm, to keep her moving. It was hard to breathe.

"Sean!" But it was barely a gasp now. She was so tired.

She never saw it coming. The water was oily black, everywhere she looked, there was no light anywhere. She couldn't see the shore. And suddenly, a wall of ice hit her, knocking her off her feet, sending her spinning, tumbling, down into the blackness.

Water rushed into her mouth, her ears, her eyes. It covered her head. She tried to reach the top, tried to push herself out of it, but there was no top. She strained to touch bottom but there was no bottom. She had walked off the edge of the shore.

The sea had her in its grip, tossing her, tugging her, turning her upside down. Her lungs were bursting. She wanted to breathe, but there was nothing to breathe. She wanted to see, struggled desperately to see, but all she saw was darkness everywhere. And cold. She couldn't fight the cold anymore.

And then it wasn't so cold. The water around her felt warmer, warm enough to make her skin tingle and her half-frozen fingers and toes prickle like pins and needles. And it wasn't dark anymore. There was a light.... All around her was light.

That was it then. She must be dying. People always talked about that bright light.

But there was something in the light, something with shape and substance. It seemed to embrace her, to take her in its arms and lift her toward the surface.

And then she knew she must be dead because as they rose out of the sea—she and the creature of light—as she burst through the surface and dragged in her first lungful of clear cold air, the face she saw above her was Sean's.

And then she saw nothing else.

SHE AWOKE aching and weak. She saw a flickering orange-gold light, smelled something wonderful and familiar. Wood smoke. She was lying in front of a fire, naked and wrapped in several layers of quilts, and a dog was sniffing at her hand.

Delilah. Molly was inside the cottage, lying before the fire, and someone was leaning over her, touching her face. Sean. She wasn't surprised.

"Am I dead?" she murmured.

"No, you little fool," he said roughly, "though you should be." He had a warm towel, and with it he began to chafe her hands and her feet. "That water is only a few degrees above freezing. You could have drowned."

He was hurting her hands, and she pulled away, letting her eyes drift closed again. She felt so sleepy. "I just had to trust my lover not to let that happen, didn't I?"

WHEN SHE WOKE AGAIN, he was still there. He was wearing jeans and a fisherman's sweater, and he sat beside her with his elbow propped against one upraised knee, fist curled against his lips. He watched her with eyes that were dark and worried.

It all came back to her. The mad flight through the darkness and the storm, the frantic search, the plunge into the sea. Could it be she, Molly Blake, who had done all this? Who had completely lost control, abandoned her senses, cast reason aside and listened to her heart?

Sean was there, and the answer was yes.

When he saw she was awake, he lowered his hand to rest against her forehead. "I'll take you upstairs in a while," he said softly. "Right now, I think you're warmer where you are, in front of the fire." He looked around the dark cottage. "There's no central heat in this place."

There was a towel wrapped around Molly's hair and a pillow beneath her head. Delilah slept at her feet, keeping them warm. The fire was toasty. Encased securely in the quilts, Molly was comfortable.

She reached for his hand. "Thank you for saving me," she said.

A shadow of remembered pain flickered across his eyes. "I thought you were afraid of the water."

She brought his hand to rest against her cheek. "I was more afraid of losing you."

His fingers tightened on hers. His lashes lowered, shielding the intensity of emotion in his eyes, but Molly could feel it, warming her like the light of the sun.

"You came back." His voice was thick, his tone tentative as though he couldn't believe the words he was uttering. Never believed he would say them. "I prayed you would come back."

"I was afraid I'd be too late."

"No." There was a catch in his voice; he cleared his throat. When he looked at her, the adoration in his eyes seemed to wash through her soul, cleansing it, setting it on fire. "You were just in time."

If ever there had been a moment's doubt about whether or not she'd made a mistake in coming back here, it was gone then. Knowing him, loving him, just being near him was worth any risk, any insanity.

"I want to stay with you, Sean. Whatever that means, whatever it takes . . . I want to stay."

"What about your job?"

She smiled. "You were right. It wasn't for me."

She lifted her hand, threading her fingers through his hair. It was soft and wavy, still a little thick with the residue of salt. "No one has ever cared for me enough to give me what I needed, not what I wanted," she told him softly. "You let me choose. You let me find out for myself."

"It wouldn't have meant anything otherwise."

With the backs of his fingers, he stroked her forehead. His touch was as magical as ever. It made her skin sing.

"And you," he said, "you sacrificed everything for me. Your job, the life you know and love—"

"That was nothing. None of those things means anything to me anymore."

"Your fear," he added gently, his eyes adoring her, "your suspicions. Even your common sense."

"Thank you for teaching me how to do that."

She took his face in both her hands and, lifting herself off the pillow slightly, she kissed his lips. It was gentle and tender and heartrendingly sweet. It was only a prelude to the beauty of what they would share in the weeks and months and years ahead.

She sank back onto the pillow, stroking his face, treating her fingertips to the texture and planes and contours of him, filling her eyes with his beauty. "You really are an oceanographer, aren't you?"

He turned her palm to his lips and kissed it gently. "I'm anything you want me to be."

"Your name is Sean Seaward and you're an oceanographer with Boston University."

He raised his eyes to hers. "Then why didn't you go looking for me in Boston?"

"Because," Molly whispered, her eyes searching his, "you are a creature of the sea and the air and I love you with all my heart."

His chest expanded with a deep breath, his lashes shadowed his eyes. His arms stretched out on either side of her, hands cupping her head. His need for her was a palpable thing that sharpened the air and thickened his voice.

"And you are the woman who made me whole. I will love you forever."

Molly's hands traced the shape of his shoulders, felt the slight tremor of the muscles of his biceps as her hands stroked him. She loved the feel of him. She loved his smell and his shape and his nearness. She wanted to be close to him, and stay close to him forever.

"Tell me a story, Sean," she said.

He smiled. "No. This time, you tell me one."

"I don't know any stories. I only know the endings."

Something in his eyes quickened and kindled, searching hers. "Then tell me the ending."

Molly threaded her fingers through his damp hair, caressing the side of his face.

"He found her," Molly said softly. "The woman he was meant to love, his mate for all time. She came to him of her own free will, and the spell that condemned him to life beneath the sea was broken. They lived together and loved each other forever."

He took her fingers and pressed them to his lips. "That," he said, "was an ending worth waiting for."

The love that flooded Molly's chest threatened to close off her throat. It brimmed in her eyes and thickened her voice as, with her free hand she caressed the back of his neck. Drawing him closer. "Take off your clothes," she whispered. "Come lie beside me."

He did.

THE LOCALS TALKED for generations of the sunrise that graced the skies that morning, spreading across the face of the sea, colors like none that had ever been seen before. They said it meant the Sea King had come home.

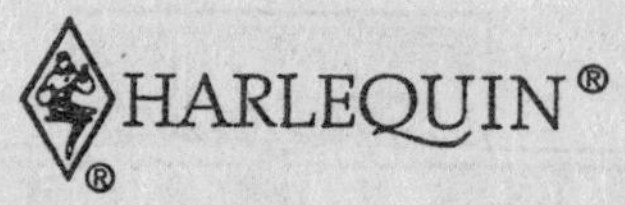

EXPECTATIONS
Shannon Waverly

Eternity, Massachusetts, is a town with something special going for it. According to legend, those who marry in Eternity's chapel are destined for a lifetime of happiness. As long as the legend holds true, couples will continue to flock here to marry and local businesses will thrive.

Unfortunately for the town, Marion and Geoffrey Kent are about to prove the legend wrong!

EXPECTATIONS, available in July from Harlequin Romance®, is the second book in Harlequin's new cross-line series, **WEDDINGS, INC.** Be sure to look for the third book, **WEDDING SONG,** by Vicki Lewis Thompson (Harlequin Temptation® #502), coming in August.

WED-2

A NEW STAR COMES OUT TO SHINE....

American Romance continues to search the heavens for the best new talent... the best new stories.

Join us next month when a new star appears in the American Romance constellation:

Rosemary Grace
#544 HONKY TONK DREAMS
July 1994

Sam Triver had heard of unusual ways to meet a woman, but never this *unusual. When he walked into the newsroom, there stood transplanted Texan Lonnie "Lone Star" Stockton—her six-guns pointed to the ceiling. It may not have been love at first sight—but you couldn't deny that sparks were flying!*

Be sure to Catch a "Rising Star"!

STAR1

INDULGE A LITTLE 6947 SWEEPSTAKES
NO PURCHASE NECESSARY

HERE'S HOW THE SWEEPSTAKES WORKS:
The Harlequin Reader Service shipments for January, February and March 1994 will contain, respectively, coupons for entry into three prize drawings: a trip for two to San Francisco, an Alaskan cruise for two and a trip for two to Hawaii. To be eligible for any drawing using an Entry Coupon, simply complete and mail according to directions.

There is no obligation to continue as a Reader Service subscriber to enter and be eligible for any prize drawing. You may also enter any drawing by hand printing your name and address on a 3" x 5" card and the destination of the prize you wish that entry to be considered for (i.e., San Francisco trip, Alaskan cruise or Hawaiian trip). Send your 3" x 5" entries to: Indulge a Little 6947 Sweepstakes, c/o Prize Destination you wish that entry to be considered for, P.O. Box 1315, Buffalo, NY 14269-1315, U.S.A. or Indulge a Little 6947 Sweepstakes, P.O. Box 610, Fort Erie, Ontario L2A 5X3, Canada.

To be eligible for the San Francisco trip, entries must be received by 4/30/94; for the Alaskan cruise, 5/31/94; and the Hawaiian trip, 6/30/94. No responsibility is assumed for lost, late or misdirected mail. Sweepstakes open to residents of the U.S. (except Puerto Rico) and Canada, 18 years of age or older. All applicable laws and regulations apply. Sweepstakes void wherever prohibited.

For a copy of the Official Rules, send a self-addressed, stamped envelope (WA residents need not affix return postage) to: Indulge a Little 6947 Rules, P.O. Box 4631, Blair, NE 68009, U.S.A.

INDR93

INDULGE A LITTLE 6947 SWEEPSTAKES
NO PURCHASE NECESSARY

HERE'S HOW THE SWEEPSTAKES WORKS:
The Harlequin Reader Service shipments for January, February and March 1994 will contain, respectively, coupons for entry into three prize drawings: a trip for two to San Francisco, an Alaskan cruise for two and a trip for two to Hawaii. To be eligible for any drawing using an Entry Coupon, simply complete and mail according to directions.

There is no obligation to continue as a Reader Service subscriber to enter and be eligible for any prize drawing. You may also enter any drawing by hand printing your name and address on a 3" x 5" card and the destination of the prize you wish that entry to be considered for (i.e., San Francisco trip, Alaskan cruise or Hawaiian trip). Send your 3" x 5" entries to: Indulge a Little 6947 Sweepstakes, c/o Prize Destination you wish that entry to be considered for, P.O. Box 1315, Buffalo, NY 14269-1315, U.S.A. or Indulge a Little 6947 Sweepstakes, P.O. Box 610, Fort Erie, Ontario L2A 5X3, Canada.

To be eligible for the San Francisco trip, entries must be received by 4/30/94; for the Alaskan cruise, 5/31/94; and the Hawaiian trip, 6/30/94. No responsibility is assumed for lost, late or misdirected mail. Sweepstakes open to residents of the U.S. (except Puerto Rico) and Canada, 18 years of age or older. All applicable laws and regulations apply. Sweepstakes void wherever prohibited.

For a copy of the Official Rules, send a self-addressed, stamped envelope (WA residents need not affix return postage) to: Indulge a Little 6947 Rules, P.O. Box 4631, Blair, NE 68009, U.S.A.

INDR93

INDULGE A LITTLE SWEEPSTAKES

OFFICIAL ENTRY COUPON

This entry must be received by: JUNE 30, 1994
This month's winner will be notified by: JULY 15, 1994
Trip must be taken between: AUGUST 31, 1994-AUGUST 31, 1995

YES, I want to win the 3-Island Hawaiian vacation for two. I understand that the prize includes round-trip airfare, first-class hotels and pocket money as revealed on the "wallet" scratch-off card.

Name____________________

Address ________________ Apt. ________

City____________________

State/Prov.____________ Zip/Postal Code__________

Daytime phone number________________
(Area Code)

Account #____________________

Return entries with invoice in envelope provided. Each book in this shipment has two entry coupons—and the more coupons you enter, the better your chances of winning!

 MONTH3

INDULGE A LITTLE SWEEPSTAKES

OFFICIAL ENTRY COUPON

This entry must be received by: JUNE 30, 1994
This month's winner will be notified by: JULY 15, 1994
Trip must be taken between: AUGUST 31, 1994-AUGUST 31, 1995

YES, I want to win the 3-Island Hawaiian vacation for two. I understand that the prize includes round-trip airfare, first-class hotels and pocket money as revealed on the "wallet" scratch-off card.

Name____________________

Address ________________ Apt. ________

City____________________

State/Prov.____________ Zip/Postal Code__________

Daytime phone number________________
(Area Code)

Account #____________________

Return entries with invoice in envelope provided. Each book in this shipment has two entry coupons—and the more coupons you enter, the better your chances of winning!

© 1993 HARLEQUIN ENTERPRISES LTD. MONTH3